THE BEGUILERS

RED FOX

Also by Kate Thompson

Switchers Trilogy

Switchers
Midnight's Choice
Wild Blood

Missing Link Series

The Missing Link
Only Human

The Alchemist's Apprentice

THE BEGUILERS

KATE THOMPSON

RED FOX Definitions

For Jane

The Beguilers
A RED FOX BOOK 0 09 941149 0

First published in Great Britain by The Bodley Head,
an imprint of Random House Children's Books

Bodley Head edition published 2001
This edition published 2002

1 3 5 7 9 10 8 6 4 2

Copyright © Kate Thompson, 2001

The right of Kate Thompson to be identified as the author of this work has been
asserted in accordance with the Copyright, Designs and Patents Act 1988.

All rights reserved. No part of this publication may be reproduced, stored in a retrieval system,
or transmitted in any form or by any means, electronic, mechanical, photocopying, recording
or otherwise, without the prior permission of the publishers.

Papers used by Random House Children's Books are natural, recyclable products
made from wood grown in sustainable forests. The manufacturing processes conform
to the environmental regulations of the country of origin.

Red Fox Books are published by Random House Children's Books,
61–63 Uxbridge Road, London W5 5SA,
a division of The Random House Group Ltd,
in Australia by Random House Australia (Pty) Ltd,
20 Alfred Street, Milsons Point, Sydney, NSW 2061, Australia,
in New Zealand by Random House New Zealand Ltd,
18 Poland Road, Glenfield, Auckland 10, New Zealand,
and in South Africa by Random House (Pty) Ltd,
Endulini, 5A Jubilee Road, Parktown 2193, South Africa

THE RANDOM HOUSE GROUP Limited Reg. No. 954009
www.**kids**at**randomhouse**.co.uk

A CIP catalogue record for this book is available from the British Library.

Printed and bound by Bookmarque Ltd, Croydon, Surrey

PART ONE

CHAPTER ONE

When I got back from the drowning pool that night there was no one around apart from Tigo, the chuffie who lives in our yard. When he heard me coming he sat up outside the hen-house door and tried to look vigilant, as though he were actively guarding the place instead of just sleeping there.

There were one or two leaf-lanterns burning in our house. It looked peaceful and inviting, but I didn't want to go in just yet in case there was someone still awake. The questions would be too awkward and I would need to be ready. I had to spend a bit more time getting myself re-orientated and clearing the dreams from my eyes.

For a while I stood looking back the way I had come, towards the mountain side, but all was dark and still. Tigo made no move towards me. He had learnt not to approach me unless I asked him. I lingered a moment longer, then decided to risk it. I would have to pay with a few sneezes and maybe worse, but I needed to share this with someone and, given the circumstances, only a chuffie would do.

Tigo stuffed his nose into my ear as I sat down beside him. Despite my allergy I like chuffies, always have, but I still wish they wouldn't do that. I wiped my ear with the end of my shawl and said, 'I've been up beside the lake. I've been watching the beguilers.'

'Phhoowow!' said Tigo and moved round to look quizzically into my face.

'There were three of them,' I said. 'One of them came really close.'

I suppose I must have been a bit more dreamy than I realised. Tigo looked worried and slopped around my face with the wettest part of his nose. I pushed him away and got up. 'The hole is in the back wall of the hen-house, Tigo. There's no point at all in sleeping beside the door.'

'Whap?' he said, indignantly.

'But you were sleeping,' I said. 'You only woke up when you heard me coming.'

'Wumbleguff sniffdoddy huffhuffhuff,' he grumbled. As he stood up and began to move around the side of the building, he gave me a wallop on the shoulder with his thick, bushy tail, accidentally-on-purpose.

'Whoops!' he said, but he didn't hang around to hear my reply. I tossed a couple of pebbles after him but they lodged in his fur and he didn't even feel them.

I stayed where I was and waited. The lights didn't necessarily mean that there was anybody still awake. My family would be sure that I was staying overnight at someone else's house, but they would still keep a few leaves burning for me and the back door unlatched. It was an old custom, laid down at some time beyond memory when it was still considered safe to go out alone after dark. No one ever did that now. Not unless they were . . .

My chain of thought was conveniently broken by a sneeze and I didn't return to it. I looked up at the sky, trying to work out what the time was. The moon was still high, still bright. On the mountain slopes there was no more sign of the beguilers. There was no knowing where they might be.

I decided to wait it out a bit longer. It would have done me no harm to have company just then; I could tell that I was still mesmerised and inclined to sink into my own dreams, following the beguilers. I wished that I hadn't offended Tigo.

He wouldn't hold it against me, chuffies never do, but I couldn't go crawling after him now.

It all began earlier that night. The moon was full and the village was holding its monthly gathering. For reasons I could never understand, most people looked forward to these meetings; anxious to hear what everyone else was up to and what their latest plans were. I seemed to be almost alone in finding them utterly tedious. And this one, I knew, was likely to be even worse than most. The summer rains had failed, for the fourth year running, and the drought was upon us again.

I could predict, almost down to the last word, what would happen at the meeting. I would have cried off; pretended to be ill, but I knew my mother wouldn't believe me and would make me pay for it all week with withering glances and stony silence.

So I went.

It started like any other meeting. I was sitting beside my younger sister, Temma, in the juvenile quarter. I was just about the oldest of the girls in that section. A girl can offer a Great Intention at any time from her fourteenth birthday onwards, which is two years before a boy can. Most of my friends couldn't wait much beyond their fourteenth birthday. The first Great Intention for a teenager means the beginning of adulthood and, for some reason that I could never quite understand, nearly all of my friends thought they wouldn't start to live until they had moved over to the next quarter, among the young men and women. But I was in no hurry.

The thing is, there are so few choices. We can't get out of here. The plains people don't like us because the way we live is peculiar to them, and the other villages that used to exist in the area have been abandoned because of the way the weather has changed. If it wasn't for the drowning pool, which provided us with water during the frequent drought, we wouldn't survive here, either. So you get married and start a family or you get married and don't start a family. That's what life amounts to. If you're unlucky you don't get married and then you might enter the priesthood. For as long as I could remember, my mind had been bashing against those paltry alternatives like a blue-bottle in a butter-box, but all I could ever come up with was the vague certainty that there had to be more to life than that.

I said it to my father once and it was a great mistake. I should have had more sense. When you're different anyway it pays to keep quiet and not spell things out for people. Since then I've kept my mouth shut, but it made me even more determined not to relent and do the normal thing. My brother Lenko felt a bit the same, I know, although we have always had problems about discussing things honestly together. He's a boy, after all, and I'm a girl. My parents didn't say it, but I know they blamed his restlessness on me. They blamed everything that went wrong in our family on me. Me and my allergy.

Anyhow, that night, the night when my life's adventure began, didn't seem any different from any other. If anyone was expecting either of us to offer up a Great Intention, they were heading for disappointment. It was warm, so my little sister Temma and I had chosen to sit as far away from the central fire as we could. We were surrounded by the other girls from the village, from the age of nine upwards. Most of them lolled about and leaned against each other, weary from a hard day's work in the forests or the fields or the kitchen. Temma had been out with two other girls watching the village goats that day, and she was almost asleep where she sat. I had to wake her up when the meeting began.

We were all supposed to be sitting in orderly rows, so that

everyone would know when it was their turn, but in fact it never worked out like that and there was often confusion about who should speak next. The Intentions began, with the youngest as usual. The only difference from the ordinary, boring old stuff was the arrival of the drought. Temma's friend Simka was the first to speak. She stood up and took the old white bone that the priestess handed to her. It was shiny from its passage through the hands of the village population for more years than anyone could remember. The priests held that it was the shinbone of the Great Mother who gave birth to our people a million years ago, but most of us believed that it had once belonged to an ox.

'I have succeeded in my last Intention,' Simka said, 'which was to bring an extra load of wood every week to my grandmother. This month I will help my family to carry water to our crops.'

The priestess bowed her head in acknowledgement and Simka passed the bone to her twin sister Anna.

'I have succeeded in my last Intention, which was to pick and preserve enough eazle-wood to clean the family's teeth for a year. This month I will help my family to carry water to our crops.'

The priestess bowed her head again and passed on. The next to speak should have been the twins' older sister, Hansa, who is about nine months younger than me, but she declined to take the bone and I knew why. She was going to offer a Great Intention, and I was fairly certain what it would be. A little further around the hall, my cousin Bick was nervously rolling and unrolling his shawl. He also intended to offer a Great Intention. Those two would speak when all the others had said their piece, along with anyone else who had a major announcement to make.

Great Intentions are made rarely in life. Once a young

member of the community has come of age, they are expected to come up with one over the next year or two. It doesn't have to be marriage, of course, although it usually is. But it has to be something that is fundamental in life, a major change, probably the biggest step that a person has ever taken. It's a serious matter to offer a Great Intention, and if it fails it can cast a shadow over the rest of your life.

Temma got up. 'I have succeeded in my last Intention, which was to sew a new dress from the material my mother gave me. This month I will help my family carry water to our crops.'

The bone was handed on. In strict order of age it was passed around the juvenile section and every voice repeated the same, monotonous intention. I fell into a moody reverie, and the sound of the meeting grew distant and echoey. And then, suddenly, it was my turn to stand and spout.

To be honest, I find the whole business ridiculous, but it is our custom and I go along with it in word, if not in spirit.

'I have failed in my last Intention,' I said. Usually people give an excuse of some kind when they fail, but I never bother. I knew that my parents didn't like it. I could feel their discomfort from the other side of the hall. I didn't know it then, but it was nothing compared to the discomfort they were going to feel in another few minutes.

I went on. 'I had intended to read and understand Chapter 17 of the Books and speak to our priests about it. My Intention for this month . . .' I stopped. I hadn't given it any thought, but the idea of blithely repeating what everyone had said was repugnant to me. It wasn't that I didn't want to help with the crisis. I did. I just couldn't say the same words.

'My Intention for this month is to spend time working out a more efficient way of getting water to our crops.'

It was something I had thought about a lot in the past. The

system we had worked all right, but it was highly labour intensive and inefficient. I was sure there had to be a better way. Sometimes my mind would manufacture strange devices, with levers and wheels and tubes. I had a theory about gravitational pull, and once I had come close to working out a system of clay pipes and sluices that I was almost sure would work. I was convinced that, with a bit more time, I could have come up with a working model. But if I had thought about it, I would never have dared to say it.

An oppressive silence fell over the hall. I handed the bone forward to the youngest of the boys in our section. It was taken from my hand, but no one spoke. The priests were still glaring at me, and so was everyone else in the congregation.

What could I do? I shouldn't have said it, I know. The traditions of the village are sacred and change is resisted rather than welcomed. And when it does happen, it is always at the behest of the elders. It is never, never instigated by the young.

If there had been a convenient hole, I would have bolted down it. But there was nowhere to hide. I was punished by the hard glare of public disapproval until I squirmed in my seat, and it wasn't until I hung my head in shame that I was released and the Intentions moved on. The boys took up from where the girls had left off. There were a lot of promises of ditch clearance, as well as more water-bearing; more conformity.

It all washed over me. My face burned with humiliation. It was highly likely that the priests would take me to one side when the meeting was over and give me a lecture; perhaps even a punishment of some kind. I tried to imagine what form it might take. A meditational penance, perhaps? Or some arduous educational task, like learning one of the ancient Epic Poems by heart?

The boys' intentions were over. Beside me, one of the younger women was promising to go up and stay with the men, to cook for them while they worked. Afterwards a series of men offered to take the oxen up to the drowning pool and spend their nights in the byre that had been built up there, and to draw water from first light until midday. It was gruelling for the men and many times worse for the beasts. We usually lost at least one ox during the drought, and sometimes more.

The voices droned slavishly on, and my shame began to turn to anger. Why shouldn't someone suggest that there might be an easier way? Even if I failed, wasn't my intention honourable?

Without a word to anyone, I slipped quietly from my seat and made my way around the back of the hall to one of the side doors. There was a pause in the Intentions, and I knew that everyone was watching me. I didn't care. I wasn't going to wait around to be castigated.

Outside the streets were empty and bright with moonlight. Above the village the mountainside looked oddly enticing and I scanned the shining darkness for signs of beguilers. The nights of the village meetings were the only times we ever went out after dark. The beguilers never came around the village when there was a full moon. No one knew why. But occasionally we would see them up among the hills as we were making our way home, dancing above the trees like huge sparks from a bonfire. It was safe to watch them then, but never at any other time of the month.

I could hear the drone of voices emerging from the hall, and it filled me with misery to think of the same old routine, the same small fulfilments and failures going round and round and round. The sound, and the thoughts that came with it, began to draw me back towards the old conundrum of what to do with my life. In an effort to shrug it all off I found myself taking the track that led out of the village and up towards the forest.

I'm still not sure whether fate is something that happens to a person or something we create for ourselves as we go along. But that night, with the full moon hanging in a cloudless sky, it seemed to me that there was nothing else in the world that I could do or that I would want to do. Despite the endless warnings that had filled my childhood nights with dread, I had no fear as I wandered up the track. It's almost as though there was something calling me and I certainly had no desire to try and resist it. I suppose that's what people mean when they talk about being summoned by fate.

CHAPTER TWO ☉

That night, when I walked up the mountain on my own, I saw three beguilers gathering on the deep lake that lies about a mile above the village. I had no warning of their presence before I saw them; they weren't keening the way they do when they come around the houses at night. They made no sound at all. One minute I was alone in the moonlight and the next minute they were there, shining out like torches in the sky.

The local wisdom is that the beguilers lose their power under the full moon. Even so, people never come out of the village at night, and the presence of the three creatures made me anxious. I turned my face away from them and walked on along the path. I wasn't far from the beginning of the forest, and my first thought was to keep going until I was safely within the trees. Then I wouldn't be tempted to look and they would forget about me. But they flew across the path in front of me and wheeled around above my head for a while before they turned again and headed back towards the lake.

There are puffberry bushes between the village and the forest, hundreds of them. When they're in fruit all the children come up at dawn every morning to pick as many as they can before the birds get to them. It's one of the best times of the year as far as I'm concerned. I'd eat puffberries until they came out of my ears. One of the best Intentions I ever thought of was to go up to that patch of hill-side every day for a month to weed out the creeping spinescutch which was growing between the bushes, choking them and making it difficult to pick the fruit. The following month several other people joined me and we had a great time working together up there. We brought all the cut creepers down to the village and made a central pile for people to use as kindling. My parents almost thought I was normal when I did that. They used to remind me of it from time to time, especially when they were particularly worried about my mood or the way I was behaving, but I think it was as much to reassure themselves as me. I had come to terms with my allergy and the way it had separated me from the other members of the community. It was they that hadn't.

But that night, when I was out walking on my own, I had no thoughts of sameness or difference, and I had no thought of puffberries, either. All I knew was that I had to take cover and refuse to see those beings that were dancing around in my path.

Beguilers. No one really knows exactly what they are because no one has ever caught one. They are around during the day but you can't see them because they have the same quality as the daylight. Occasionally, if you're up on the mountain slopes, you might see a shadow pass through the air like a wafer of ice floating on water; not quite substantial enough to be sure that it's really there. But at dusk they become visible, and at night they are as bright and vivid as huge fireflies.

Some people say that they are demons drawn down from the cloud mountain to feed on human souls. Others say that they are the earth-bound spirits of wayfarers who lost their lives in the mountains and who need to lead another soul to a similar death before they can be freed from their torment. Because tormented they certainly are. The sound of their moaning, howling voices floating through the village streets in the darkness would freeze the blood in your heart.

However hot the night might be, we close our shutters when we hear them coming and wrap our shawls around our ears.

We are warned never to peep out at them from the first day we can understand the words. We are told that they are beautiful, so beautiful that people become mesmerised by them and get led astray. There are endless stories about them; of people who succumbed to the lure of their haunted voices and walked out into the night, never to be seen again; or got caught in the darkness between one place and another and didn't return home. Every accident that happens on the mountain is blamed on the beguilers. Every time a traveller is lost on the road or falls down a precipice, the elders tell us that it was because they were following a beguiler. Our people live in terror of darkness; after nightfall we are prisoners in our own homes, waiting for the haunting voices to draw us from our sleep. It is one of the reasons that we are so isolated. Apart from the porters who have to pass through our village, carrying goods across the mountains to the coastal communities on the other side, we have no regular visitors at all.

I suppose I never really believed the stories. The beguilers are eerie all right; they're eerie to look at and eerie to hear, but aside from that I had never heard any real evidence that they interacted with people at all. They were a convenient excuse, though, for the fears that people have of the darkness. I always thought that if it wasn't beguilers it'd be something else, another kind of spook designed to keep children at home in bed. There hadn't been an accident in all the time that I was alive, or at least not one that could realistically be attributed to a beguiler. I had always had a secret fascination for the night and chafed against the customs of the village. But now, alone on the mountain with those strange and silent creatures, I wasn't so sure.

I lay down on my stomach among the puffberry bushes

and put my hands over my eyes. I couldn't hear them, but I could sense them some other way, still flitting about above my head. At least, I believed I could. There was no question of my being in any danger unless I looked at them; of that I was sure. The legends say that it is only when you look into the eyes of a beguiler they become a danger to you. Even so, I was afraid. There's no sense in pretending that I wasn't.

I kept my eyes covered for as long as I could. With my head there close to the ground I thought at first that the world was filled with some enormous noise, appropriate to the fear that I was experiencing. But before long I realised that the sound I was hearing was the sound of fear itself. My heart was pounding, causing the blood to roar in my ears, and my rapid breathing was amplified because my face was pressed against the ground. When I relaxed for a moment and held my breath, I found that the world was almost silent.

I became aware of the night insects in the grass among the bushes, and a stray creeper of spinescutch was pricking into my stomach. I moved a hand to pull it away and saw only darkness all around. Carefully I looked up. The beguilers were gone. Slowly, cautiously, I got to my feet and looked out. Far below, the soft lights of the village were visible but that was all.

The moonlight was cool and distant, comfortless. As my fear subsided and my circulation returned to normal and was forgotten, I realised that my knees were trembling. What had happened to me there on the mountain was one of the most frightening experiences of my life, but it was also one of the most exhilarating. Even as I stood there with the sweat of fear cooling beneath my shirt, I was aware of an authenticity within, a correspondence of circumstance with my own nature.

If I had assumed anything while I lay among the puffberry

bushes it was that if I survived the ordeal I would return straight home. But now I had no desire to do so. The faint, twinkling lights of the village were not suggestive of comfort but of suffocation and retribution. Whatever had brought me up on to the hill-side in the darkness had not been weakened by my encounter with the beguilers, but strengthened instead. With little sense of purpose but with a great sense of freedom, I turned away from the village.

The particular formation of land where our village is built is called Ambarka, which means 'The lap of the Great Mother' in the old language. It's like a bulge; a lap is a fairly good description if you think of the flat part at the top of the hill where the village stands as the 'Mother's' thighs. Above the village and below it, the mountainside is steep, almost sheer in some places. The path has been made to zig-zag across the steepest parts but even so it is a stiff climb. I had gone about half a mile and was just passing a pile of rough planks that my father and Lenko had been cutting together at the edge of the forest when the beguilers returned.

They took me by surprise, sweeping across my vision again in a triangular formation, their long, translucent tails fanned out behind them like comets. Involuntarily I followed them with my eyes and then, before I knew it, I was following them with my feet as well towards the lake.

The drowning pool we call it. It is a dark and dangerous place, a hole made by a meteorite in the side of the mountain which forms a natural reservoir. It is fed by an underground stream that comes straight down from the melting end of one of the glaciers, and it is never empty. When it has been dry for a while, the sides of the pool are sheer, more frightening than when the pool is full because they go down for such a long way before they reach the water. And a long way afterwards as well, people say. Huge leather buckets on thick ropes are lowered down the sides. The ropes are slung over a frame made of stout timber, which is designed so that when the buckets are pulled by the oxen to the top, they tilt and pour their contents into the series of ditches and aqueducts that run down towards the village pond.

From there, in the cool of evening, the water has to be carried by yak or donkey or bucket-pole to the fields, some of which are nearly a mile from the houses. The whole village is involved in that part of the operation. Even the smallest child is busy, watering the crops with a small jug, until every plant that we own has been given enough to keep it alive. And the whole process goes on, every second or third day, for as long as the drought lasts. In a bad year, that could be weeks.

But the strange thing is that no matter how much water we draw from the drowning pool it is never empty. My father says that you wouldn't empty it in a hundred years. He says it is bottomless.

And now the beguilers were leading me towards it.

CHAPTER THREE

I knew that I was being lured but I wasn't mesmerised, or at least I believed that I wasn't. I was sure that I could stop as soon as I wanted to and turn back. But at least one of the things we had been told about the beguilers was true; they were the most beautiful creatures I had ever seen. Even as I followed them I was beginning to get whisperings of what was to become the first Great Intention of my life.

They were quite some distance ahead of me and I couldn't see them clearly, just their shapes in the night sky, their oval bodies and long, flowing tails. I was careful, as careful as I've ever been, keeping my eyes more often on the ground than on the strange activity in the sky. I knew the area well. There was a sort of rough track that led out of the puffberry bushes and on to the scrubby hill that sloped up towards where the lake was. Sometimes the older boys and girls gave Intentions to bring the herd there to graze the razor grass and goat-cabbage. It was a long time since man or beast had been lost to the lake, but I knew that parents were worried all the same, and in the loneliness up there that night I had more understanding of why. Taking my eyes from the moving lights that were guiding me, I cut across the steep and bumpy scrubland until I found the herders' path, and once I had reached it I resolved not to leave it.

The beguilers seemed to be made of light but, strangely, they cast none out around them. The moon was my only torch and I was lucky that it was bright enough for my needs that night. I stayed on the track even when the beguilers veered away and approached the lake from the top end where the side of the mountain slopes steeply down and drops into the hole. That was the most dangerous part, I knew. Even the most courageous youths didn't venture up there. One slip and you'd had it, rolling down the hill-side and straight into mid-air above the dark water. I stayed on course and stopped at the top of the path near the ox-byre. Then I lay down on my belly and crawled to the edge. Below me the sides of the pool were sheer and the lake was black, as though the water was so dark that it couldn't reflect the moonlight at all but could go on absorbing it for ever and ever. I had balanced myself so that if I slipped at all it would be backwards, but even so I held tight to a stalk of goat-cabbage with each hand. The beguilers were gathered together at the top end of the lake. They were hovering above the water and moving around in an aimless sort of circular dance the way nippers do, dipping now and then to touch the water as if they were fishing for something. What was strange though, a bit creepy, was that even though they appeared to touch the water, they never made any ripples. The surface of the lake was as still as a slab of gloss-rock.

After a while I realised that they were moving closer, towards my side of the lake. They were still beneath me, and I looked directly down on them as they took up their strange flight pattern again.

There are some creatures called waterpods that we used to play with in the ditches after the rains. They are completely transparent except for their eyes and their digestive systems. It makes me feel sick to think of it now, but we used to aim them at each other and burst the poor things. I remembered them as I watched the beguilers dancing because there was something similar about them. Mostly they were just light, and mostly you felt that you could see straight through them if it wasn't darker on the other side. That's true, I think, and that's the reason that you can't see them during the day. But there is a suggestion of something more substantial about them, of something not quite seen, and that is what intrigued me about them and made me strain my eyes against the night. They were infuriating, always moving so that I couldn't quite see, and leaving irritating trails of light to evaporate behind them, insubstantial as steam.

I don't know to this day whether or not the beguilers were aware of me watching them, but at the time I didn't think about it at all because I was so fascinated. They moved away a short distance, still dancing, still dropping towards the water now and again so that I wondered if they might possibly be feeding on something in there. I had realised by now that they were making a full circuit of the lake, round the edge from one side to the other. As they moved further away it was even more difficult to see them and I closed my eyes for a while to rest them from the strain of trying to see something that couldn't be seen. When I opened them again, the beguilers were still there, just about completing their circuit of the drowning pool.

The air was warm on my back. I closed my eyes again, and a blissful sleepy sensation trickled through me. It would have been so easy to go to sleep there, as warm and comfortable as in my bed at home. But something jerked me awake again. Perhaps it was some sound that the beguilers made or perhaps it was the movement of their light outside my lids. They must have gathered in the centre of the lake, for suddenly they were sweeping off in different directions up out of the bowl. And one was coming straight towards me.

I was wide awake now and my eyes were glued to the flying light. It rose swiftly, gracefully, up in front of my eyes and then up above my head and over me. Despite myself I turned on to my back to follow its flight, and when it was directly above my face it stopped and hovered in the air.

Now I could see it, the beauty that hypnotised people. Now that the creature was no longer in motion the light had ceased bleeding out from behind it and seemed to be concentrated at its centre. The substance that I had been straining to see was almost apparent as it looked down upon me with unmistakable curiosity in its eyes. Yes, its eyes; it did have eyes. They were mellow and deep; golden concentrations of pure light or pure heat, fire refined and compacted into two bright globes which looked straight down upon me. Exactly what was in those eyes I will never know, but what I saw was a number of things. There was curiosity as strong as my own, but also pain and longing and a need to be understood. Those were all qualities that were familiar to me, the visual equivalent of the tormented cries that I had heard so many times. That was disturbing, of course, but what was even more disturbing to me was the certainty that the being that hovered above me was familiar. I had encountered it before somewhere. The eyes that looked down on me were not human in origin, but nevertheless they were known to me, in some other form, the way someone might not be themselves in a dream but you know it is them all the same.

There was no point in reaching out with my hands, I knew that. The beguiler was too far above me. But I reached out with my mind, pleading, grasping, imploring it to come down to me. I hadn't known it before, but somehow I learned at that moment that being human was painful; a thing to be pitied.

And was it scorn that I saw in its eyes as it turned in the air above me and soared away so effortlessly? Perhaps, perhaps not. But its action seemed to me to be scornful, to leave me there helplessly bound to the ground while it defied all the laws that the mountain imposed upon the rest of us.

I lay still long after the beguiler had disappeared. And while I lay there a decision was made. I suppose that I have to say it was I who made the decision, although it seems strange when I recall how hard I tried to persuade myself to change it over the next month. I began to try and change it that very night, even as I got up and started to walk home. I told myself that I was crazy, that no one had ever succeeded in such an undertaking and no one ever would. I told myself that I was lucky to be alive and that if I carried on with this crazy plan I certainly wouldn't be for very much longer. But it made no difference. My mind was made up.

CHAPTER FOUR

I didn't tell Tigo about my Great Intention, but from the way he looked at me over the next weeks I've a fair suspicion that he guessed. I didn't tell anyone else, either. One of the rules about Intentions is that they must never be revealed to anyone before they are made public. In the case of a Great Intention, you're supposed to discuss all the alternatives with your parents or the elders, but there's nothing anyone can do if you don't. And once you have offered your Great Intention, there's no going back. You can change your own mind if you think you could live with yourself, but no one else can change your mind for you and they won't try. It's your life; your decision.

The other thing, though, and it was one of the things I kept telling myself when I was trying to change my mind, is that the announcement of the first Great Intention marks the end of your parents' responsibility for you. All the villagers are totally dependent upon each other; the village wouldn't survive if they weren't. But from the time we are nine years old we are encouraged to know our own capabilities and to be as independent as possible. That's one of the reasons for the Intention sessions every month. When children first go to them they make all kinds of crazy announcements. They think they can do anything and everything. But once they've had a few colossal failures they begin to get wise and lower their expectations of themselves. That way, by the time they come to offer their first Great Intention they're supposed to have a pretty good idea of what they can or can't do, which is why other people don't interfere.

Things go wrong, of course. Lenko's friend Samsy announced that he was going to marry his sweetheart, Diamsa, without consulting her on the matter. All their parents were furious, and he's still trying to persuade her that she wants him. It has become a bit of a village joke, like old Hemmy announcing every month that her Intention is to prepare for her death. Everyone knows that, sooner or later, Diamsa will marry Samsy. And sooner or later, of course, old Hemmy will die. Those failed Intentions aren't the end of anyone's world.

But if things went wrong for me . . . I thought about it, night after night as I lay in bed. I don't know why it was that I couldn't change my mind. It might have been that the beguilers had put me under some kind of spell already. Or it might have been an inner stubbornness, a determination not to be like everyone else even if it meant walking myself into a mess that would last for the rest of my life. Or walking myself into a mess that would bring a short end to it.

The way Tigo looked at me, that's what he thought, anyway. My allergy meant that we couldn't have chuffies in the house the way everyone else did, because if I was in an enclosed space with one my watering eyes and sneezes progressed to a full-blown attack of asthma and I had to be taken out on to the mountainside until I could breath again. People had got pretty much used to me, but from time to time, even then, someone would cast aspersions about ours being an unhappy household because of there being no chuffies in it; and then the whole business of me being different from everyone else would rear its ugly head again. They all thought I was suffering desperately, you see, because I couldn't spend half my life snuggled up with a chuffie the way other people do. And I suppose that in some ways I did suffer more than the others. The thing is, though, I never saw it as a bad thing the way they do. It's not the end of the world to feel sad or disappointed now and then. It doesn't feel nice, but it proves that you're alive and growing and changing in a way that you're hardly aware of when the chuffies snuff everything out and make you feel good. And if things got intolerable I could always go out and spend a few minutes with Tigo, and that would take care of the worst of it. I liked to sit with him in the yard from time to time in any case. He was my friend, even if he did make me sneeze. When I was really confused about the beguiler thing I liked to go out and lean against him so that he could feel how I was feeling. Chuffies understand everything. But that's not the same thing as approving. He thought I was nuts, and the way things are in our village and always have been, I had to agree with him.

Because stating that your Great Intention is to catch a beguiler is the equivalent of admitting insanity. I wasn't the first to try it, not by a long shot. On average there is one in every generation who does it and they are spoken about in hushed, disapproving tones on long, leaf-lantern evenings in the warm fug of winter fires. It's a sort of an idiom around here; if someone isn't behaving according to the local ethics, or if someone gets a bit over-wrought about something, what the others say is, 'He ought to watch out, that one. The next thing is he'll be off hunting beguilers.' My mother said it to me, once. 'You calm down, young lady, or it's off after beguilers you'll be.' Maybe she shouldn't have said that. Maybe it put the idea into my head.

It didn't matter, though, where the notion came from. I had no respect for the things that the other people were doing. I would rather have died hunting beguilers than capitulated and entered an unwanted marriage or the dusty old priesthood. After all, what's the point of being human and having choices in life if everyone just ends up behaving like cattle?

There were two names in my lifetime that were associated with beguilers. The first was Dabbo. He came to the village from time to time, I'm told, but I don't remember him. He died when I was young. The other name was Shirsha. She wasn't dead, but lived on her own in the Lepers' caves beside the were-forest, just below the snow-line. People came across her now and then. They said that she was mad, without a doubt. They shuddered when they mentioned her name. I preferred not to think about her.

Instead I tried to turn my mind to the water problem. Each evening when the household tasks were finished, I sat alone with a few scraps of paper, trying to put my theories into some sort of practical form. I produced all kinds of fascinating sketches, but none of them were close to working designs. On the evenings when we watered the crops I sometimes became immersed in my speculations, and would watch the water pouring from the spout of my can, so absorbed by the possibilities that I forgot why I was there. Eventually my father got so angry that he made me carry the bucket pole across my shoulders for a few trips. I realised then that, although the priests hadn't called me in after my insolent Intention at the meeting, they had almost certainly spoken to my parents. They would have been advised to try and turn my thoughts away from their rebellious path.

The bucket pole certainly had the effect of focussing my mind. But it set it, even more firmly, on the Great Intention I meant to make.

Despite the tiring work I was sleeping very little, tossing and turning all through the nights, listening to Lenko snoring, arguing with myself. I got so tired that my mind did get a bit blurry round the edges, and that didn't help matters because I kept catching myself with strange thoughts and wondering if the elders weren't right; if it wasn't a kind of madness to attempt what I was going to do. No one else had ever succeeded, after all. They said that very few of those who had gone off beguiler-hunting had ever come back. They, like all kinds of other unfortunates, had been led into caves in the ground or over the edges of precipices or up above the snow-line where they perished in the cold. But it was hard for me to imagine the cold when it was blisteringly hot in our village. It was also hard for me to imagine disaster.

The many times that I had neglected to carry out an Intention in the past didn't feel like failures to me. If I hadn't done what I had said I would, it was because I couldn't be bothered, not because I wasn't equal to it. I knew it was arrogant but I really believed that there was nothing I couldn't do. I believed it right up until the time that I came to announce my Great Intention at the next meeting.

The whole of the night before I lay awake, listening to the soft wind that blustered through the peppernut trees outside my window. Now and then a warm, friendly breath of it nipped into the room and told me which direction it was blowing from. It had come across the dried-up marshes and become flavoured with water-rose, and after that it had come through the orchard and picked up all the scents of the fading fruit blossoms. I remember thinking how strange it was that the flowers of those trees smelled nothing like the fruit. Their scent was something you might drink, but never eat.

That warm wind which blew in across the marshes was rare. Some of the old people say that it is a bad omen. They say that the East wind pushes the rain-bearing West wind back on to the other side of the mountain and away towards the sea. It's supposed to be dangerous to cross the pass in such conditions, because the two winds do battle there and might throw a traveller who got in their way out over the precipice.

No one believes it much, not these days. No one believes

the other thing the old people say about the East wind, either, which is that it brings failure to all Great Intentions that are offered during its passage. But I couldn't stop thinking about it, all through the night when I couldn't sleep.

On the other side of the room Lenko was snoring like a family of buzz-bats. On another night, I couldn't have stood it. I would have thrown a sandal at him or got up and pinched his nose. It was safe to do that at night because he never woke, just turned over and carried on sleeping. In the day-time it was different. Being the alleged cause of Lenko's foul temper I was seldom allowed to forget it.

But that night he could snore to his heart's content. There was no chance of me sleeping in any case. None at all. In a few hours it was going to be morning and, a few hours after that, it would be time to announce my Great Intention.

CHAPTER FIVE

At the meeting everyone was exhausted, and before the proceedings had begun several of the younger children were already fast asleep. But I was far too nervous to relax.

The Intentions began; a bland repeat of last month's meeting. It made my skin crawl. I wished that I had produced some worthwhile water scheme to prove that I wasn't just a dreamer, and I was still wondering if I might give some explanation of my lines of thought when it came to my turn.

The priestess was standing there with her hands on her hips, looking up at me. I jumped, snatched the bone from the last speaker, and was about to stand up when I remembered that Great Intentions are always offered at the end of the section. I would have to wait until the boys had finished. I passed the bone and smiled weakly at the priestess, who looked at me a little oddly and moved on. But very few of my friends and relatives heard what the first of the boys had to say. They were all looking at me.

I didn't dare look at my parents. It was unheard of to offer a Great Intention without consulting them. I could feel their eyes boring into me from the other side of the fire and I kept my face turned down. The voices around the hall droned on, the boys making the expected promises. I didn't listen to any more. I looked down at my feet, noticing for the first time that my sandals were getting too small for me and wondering how long it was since I last washed between my toes. Temma was trying to get my attention but I refused to be drawn. I was suddenly tired, and sick of the droning voices. It was absurd to be here and making crazy promises. I wished I had stayed at home with the chuffie.

After a while my thoughts were interrupted by another silence, a longer one this time. I looked up, wondering what was causing it, and saw that the priestess had come back to me. My blood ran cold. Her eyes were worn and patient but not forgiving. I was already disrupting the meeting, even before I said what I had come here to say.

Someone pushed the bone between my rigid fingers. I stood up. My mouth felt dry and incompetent as though it were stuffed with a piece of old rag.

'I wish to offer . . .' The words sounded indistinct and distant. I cleared my throat and started again. 'I wish to offer my first Great Intention.'

Foolishly, I allowed my eyes to slide round the hall and they met those of my mother. She was staring at me with a horrified expression on her face. Beside her my father had hidden his face behind his hands. I almost failed. I almost backed away and sat down again, but something else within me acted first.

'My Intention is to spend as much of my life as is necessary to seek out and catch a beguiler.'

The clarity, the certainty in my voice surprised me as much as anyone else in the hall. The silence that followed was as heavy and as perfect as the first winter snow and, like the snow, it was both magnificent and terrifying.

'You always want to be the centre of attention,' my mother used to say to me. If it was true, if that really was what I wanted, I achieved it at that moment. But if I felt that it was glorious, that feeling was short-lived. The priestess nodded and turned her back. No one else in the village was announcing a Great Intention that day, so our section was finished. Beside us, in the young adult section, people were passing the babies from lap to lap, ready for their turns. I sat down and as I did so, my head felt as though it would burst. I didn't look at my mother's expression but I could feel it anyway, the way you know what a chuffie is feeling when you lie up against him. Her rage and shame were beaming across the fire at me. No matter what happened she would never forgive me for this.

I wasn't sure whether I would be able to forgive myself, either. The spell of the beguilers had worn thin and any glamour or romance that I had associated with my search had dissolved. What I was left with was the stark and unnerving knowledge that I had just effectively cast myself out from the protection of the village. The day before I had been a slightly eccentric young woman, probably destined for the priesthood. Now, abruptly, I was mad, not to be trusted, and certainly heading straight towards my own doom. Some of the people would probably be relieved, believing that if the age had already claimed its beguiler-hunter then the other children of the village would turn out normal enough. What was harder for me to bear was the sympathy that others would feel. 'Poor girl,' they would say. 'You would never have believed it, would you? She seemed so bright when she was younger. Never entirely normal, I suppose, but you wouldn't have expected that she would go as far off track as that.'

The anger that these thoughts produced was probably all that kept me from melting into a quivering jelly right there in the hall. I didn't know why, and it certainly didn't make the kind of sense that it had before I started, but I had done it. Around me the meeting droned on, Intention after Intention, voice after voice. But I didn't hear any of it; not one single word. The same thought was circling my mind, over and over again. I had taken the plunge and announced my Intention. Now there was no going back.

CHAPTER SIX

The priests vanished quietly through their own door into the small room at the back where they would disrobe and return to the status of ordinary citizens until they were next required to work or give advice. The order of the hall broke up as families rejoined each other and neighbours gathered to gossip. I caught a glimpse of my mother moving in my direction but I stayed where I was. The others around me, those who had been my friends, moved away from me quietly, seeking a safe distance before beginning their exclamations of astonishment. Temma sat silently beside me in a sort of resigned loyalty. I appreciated it, small gesture though it was. You choose your friends after all but you can't choose your family.

After a while, I saw my mother again and, as I had anticipated, her face was already drenched with tears. She had been waylaid by her best friend Meeta and one or two other women who were no doubt offering her their sympathy and advice. Already the village chuffies were beginning to arrive and gather round the small group, drawn by the unusually high level of distress. Meeta turned her head and shot me a look of vicious scorn which hit me with almost physical impact. She had been like an aunt or a godmother to me but there would be no more sour-blossom tea for me in her house.

I thought of making an immediate departure, and I might have done if it hadn't been for old Hemmy who came hobbling across to me with the aid of her knobbly bullsback walking sticks. She stood at the bottom of the climbing tiers of benches, freed her right hand carefully from its stick and waved at me. At first I thought that she was making an angry gesture of some sort, her ancient equivalent of shaking her fist. I suppose that was all I expected from anyone. But it wasn't that. She was beckoning me down to her. Temma nudged me in the ribs, thinking I hadn't seen. I nodded and began to climb down.

People were making their way out of the wide, ornamented doors at the front of the hall. Those who passed me as I went down pretended that I wasn't there or that they hadn't seen me. It wasn't particularly pleasant, but it was preferable to Meeta's kind of response. Across on the other side of the hall I could barely see my mother for the shoving crowd of chuffies, driven frantic by the desire to get close to her and soak up her anguish. I looked down at my feet, suddenly aware of my tiredness and stress and the strange sense of disorientation that they were causing. The last thing I wanted to do now was to fall and make a fool of myself.

Hemmy's hand was back on the stick. It had been quite a feat of co-ordination for her to balance on one, and I was intrigued to know why she had made such an effort to summon me.

'Hello, Hemmy,' I said. 'Were you calling?'

'Of course I was calling you, child.'

I smiled rather foolishly and waited. After a minute or two she said, 'Didn't you hear?'

'Hear what?'

'My Intention?'

I looked at her blankly, trying to imagine what her Intention could have been, apart from yet again preparing herself for her death. She scowled at me and raised her elbow in an unmistakable gesture. I took the bullsback stick from her right hand and linked my arm in hers. Then, slowly and painstakingly, we made our way out of the meeting hall and through the crowd that had gathered outside the door.

'Gossiping,' said Hemmy, purposefully loud. I kept my eyes averted but I could feel the attention that was coming my way from all those people. It made the hair tingle on my scalp.

We crawled on, Hemmy and I, every step a major undertaking. It was as though all her old joints were seized and she had to swing her legs along without bending anything. After each step she came to a brief halt, as though gathering strength for the next one, so when she actually did stop it was some time before I realised.

We had left the crowds behind and were standing in the middle of the market street. There were only two markets here a year, one in the spring and one in the autumn when people came from all over the area to buy our goods and to sell us those things that we couldn't provide for ourselves. I always dreaded those times, mostly because the village filled up with chuffies looking for work, and although it made everyone in the area extremely good-humoured, it was murder for me with my allergy.

But that night the street was empty apart from Jeppo's goat who cleared up the peelings from his fritter stall every day. Since he did a great trade with the porters who passed through, she was fat and sleek, her udder larger and fuller than any other goat in the village. She was dozing in the corner beside the closed shutters of the stall. I spoke to her while I waited for Hemmy to get her breath back, but she shook her head so that her long ears slapped together then stretched herself out on her side to ease her bloated gut.

I must have made an impatient gesture of some kind because Hemmy snatched her arm from me and reached out for her stick, which I wedged quickly under her hand before she began to topple. A buzz-bat zipped down and snapped up a nipper from right under her nose, but she didn't even blink.

'My Intention,' she said, 'was to give you a good start in your quest.'

My heart, which had been numb since my turn to speak at the meeting, came to life again. At least there was one person in the world who was on my side. I felt tears begin to heat my eyes and I swallowed hard. It was lucky for me that most of the village chuffies were back at the meeting-hall attending to my mother.

'Well?' she said.

'Thanks, Hemmy.'

She began to totter forward again and I took her arm. As we made our way across the village to her house, people from the meeting overtook us on their way home, but no one spoke. It didn't seem to matter to me any more that our journey took so long. Hemmy had stuck her old neck out for me and I was willing to do anything for her.

As we turned into her street a chuffie came bounding towards us. Risking her balance, Hemmy waved a stick at him but it didn't stop his advance.

'Shoo,' she shouted at him. 'Go away, you stupid beast.'

The chuffie lolloped up to us and turned himself round so that his rear end was right in front of Hemmy. She stopped and tried to hit him with her stick but she was too feeble to make much impression.

'He's the most stupid chuffie that ever lived with me,' she said. 'He wants to help me along and he has this idea that I can ride on his back. But whenever he gets near me he knocks me over and I have to lie there and wait until someone comes along to help me up.'

'Why don't you sack him?' I said.

The chuffie looked at me belligerently.

'Why do you do it?' I asked him.

'Kersnaffle hopple,' he said.

'Of course I can't ride!' Hemmy yelled at him. 'I'm ninety-seven years old and my legs have seized up!'

'Humph!' said the chuffie, and trotted on ahead to open the door.

'He can be useful at home,' said Hemmy as we followed at her snail's pace. 'He brings in wood and water and he takes messages when he remembers them. He just can't get it into his head that I have to take my time, that's all.'

We walked a little further, then she said, 'Besides. An old woman without chuffies is in great danger. There's little else left in the world that can raise her spirits in the same way.'

I nodded. At times like that I regretted my allergy. If I lived to be old I might be lonely.

Hemmy's house had once been rather grand. She and her husband had not had children, but when they first married they had expected to and had built several rooms around the central part of the house. But one by one they had fallen into disrepair and the rain had washed away the walls. Now the house looked a bit like a honeycomb from the outside with just the round shells of the old rooms remaining. Their inner doors had all been closed off or made into windows and Hemmy lived, cooked and slept in the large, circular room in the middle.

The chuffie had revived the fire for our arrival and was bringing a pot of water from the well. I took it from him and settled it on the clay funnel above the flames. Hemmy lowered herself carefully on to a pile of mattresses which fitted snugly between the fire and the wall. She was too stiff to cross her legs, so she propped herself up with cushions and quilts and let out a great sigh. Her other chuffie, an old, smelly creature with a coat like a mountain goat, got up from where she had been sleeping in the corner and walked stiffly over.

The poor creature was clearly worn out, and had nothing left of her youthful exuberance. But the attachment between her and Hemmy was still strong, and if the old chuffie had not had something still to give, she would not be there. I watched as she climbed on to the cushions and propped herself firmly against Hemmy's side.

There was nothing unusual about the relationship between them, but there was something about it that moved me all the same and started my heart on a new descent. I sat on the hearth-rug, remembering what had happened and what I was doing here. Immediately the young chuffie came bounding over, knocking over a pile of empty pots as he came, and prodded my cheek with his wet nose. I tried to send him off, I really did, but my sadness was like a magnet to him. I tried explaining that it wasn't appropriate, that I was allergic to him and that in any case it was right for me to be feeling sad in the circumstances, but I might as well have been talking to the wall. He glued himself to my side and wouldn't move until he had succeeded in lifting my mood. Then he jumped up beside Hemmy despite all her protests and draped himself over her stiff old legs.

We sat quietly until the water began to hiss, then Hemmy instructed me on how to make her special whisker-fruit brew. She had a huge block of lace-tree sugar and I kept adding shavings from it until the tea turned brown. I'm not sure that it wasn't the best brew I've ever tasted. Hemmy told me to mix a bit of it with milk for the chuffies. The younger one slurped up his share, but the old one refused to come down from Hemmy's side. Instead she let out a long, low moan, which told me better than any words how far down an old woman's spirits can fall when she gets tired and how much effort it can take to lift them up again. I handed the old chuffie a couple of the dried whisker-fruit and she sucked them noisily for the rest of the evening. The younger one returned to Hemmy's lap, and she rested her tea on his broad, hairy back. He must have been quite a weight on her legs, but she didn't seem to notice it.

If Hemmy knew of my allergy she made no allowances for it. I'm not sure it would have made any difference if she had, because I couldn't imagine any way of getting that chuffie off her legs. So when my eyes began to itch I just had to put up with it.

When she had finished her brew, Hemmy handed me the empty glass and said, in a voice which creaked and scraped like her arthritic limbs, 'I nearly went once, you know?'

'Went where?'

'On your journey. To catch a beguiler.'

'Really?'

'Yes. It's one of the reasons that your parents are happy enough to leave you in my care tonight. They think that I will talk you out of this nonsense.'

The first glimmer of suspicion entered my mind. 'And will you?' I asked.

'Not if I can help it.'

'Why didn't you go?' I said, between a succession of sneezes. 'What made you change your mind?'

'Doubts. But they wouldn't have been enough on their own.' She ran a hand through her sparse hair, which would have been white if it hadn't been stained a dingy yellow by liver-wood smoke. It was a gesture which recalled the vanity of youth.

'A young man held me back,' she went on. 'Bream Yolper.'

Simultaneously, the two chuffies sighed and turned to me with exasperated expressions as though I was confounding all their efforts. Hemmy's unhappy and childless marriage to the handsomest young man of her generation was no secret in the village. The younger chuffie sighed again and wrapped a despairing paw over his nose as if to block out any more interference from outside.

'If I had it over to do again,' said Hemmy, 'I'd do what you're about to do, no matter how it turned out.'

'Would you?'

'Yes. Because I was unfulfilled. I'm ninety-seven years old and nothing in my life has measured up to my expectations. I can't even manage to die according to plan, as you may have noticed.'

Hemmy's words were mellowed by a humorous glint in her eye, and the chuffies, who had gone quite rigid as she spoke, relaxed again.

'I know why, though, now,' she went on. 'I ought to have known all along.'

'Why?' I said.

'Because I have some things to give you, to help you on your way.'

'Have you? What things?'

'I could show you if it wasn't for this dim-witted creature.' Hemmy tugged at the young chuffie's shaggy coat, but he was as inert as a crumpled rug. 'I'll have to get some sleep before I have a chance of moving him.' She looked across at me and her face showed the first signs of sympathy that I had ever seen on it. 'And so will you,' she said.

I nodded, and a great wave of exhaustion washed over me as though it had been waiting for her permission to rise. I looked around me at the jumble of pots and pans and food containers that made up Hemmy's existence. In the furthest corner from the fire was a single mattress with a pile of folded quilts at one end. From the layer of moulted hair on the mattress I guessed that it was the chuffies' bed, and if I tried to sleep there I would be desperate for breath within an hour.

Instead I picked up two of the quilts.

'Do you mind if I sleep outside?' I said, breaking into another series of fierce sneezes as though to illustrate my reason.

Hemmy nodded. Then she manoeuvred herself into a lying position with the chuffies snuggled up close beside her, and it seemed to me that she was asleep before she stopped moving.

I wandered out to the edge of the village before I went to bed, on the off-chance of seeing my beguilers again. A group of porters were camped there and I could hear them snoring inside their light tents. Beneath the full moon the snowy peaks which rose so sheer above me shone like rare metals in the sky. I could even see the shapeless top of the cloud mountain, which is usually only visible on the clearest of spring and autumn days. It seemed right that I could see it, somehow, a phenomenon as vague and unknown as the future that awaited me.

I was still gazing at it, wondering what it could be, when a voice came out of the darkness, sending a shrill shock through my bones.

'Hello?'

I looked around but I could see no one. 'Hello?'

'Are you the one?' said the voice.

I saw him, then. A young porter, lying on his back at the edge of the encampment, barely ten yards from where I stood. He was nestled among bulging sacks of rice and millet, and it was no surprise that I hadn't seen him earlier. I took a step closer. The boy was gazing up at the skies. His arms were folded beneath his head, and their undersides were white and soft in the darkness, giving an impression of vulnerability, like a lizard's belly. The nippers must have been feasting off his blood, but he was as still as the moon above.

'Am I what?' I answered.

'I heard that someone had made an Intention. To go after a beguiler. Is it you?'

His face was hidden by the moon-shadows cast by the tents, but I could imagine the scorn that would undoubtedly be written upon it.

'What if it is?' I said.

He propped himself up on his elbow and faced me, but I couldn't make out his features or his expression. I flushed, aware of a desire to sneer at him and make mad faces, to prove his suspicions were well-founded. But another thought struck me.

'Why are you outside? Aren't you afraid of the beguilers?'

His voice was soft and a bit creaky, on the edge of breaking. 'Not a bit. I wish you the best of luck.'

I wanted to ask him more. Of all the people who had cause to move about in the mountains, the porters were the most superstitious. I had never encountered anyone, anywhere, sleeping out in the open at night, even beneath the full moon. From inside one of the tents, an irritable voice called out to him to be quiet and go to sleep. He shrugged at me, then turned on to his side and pulled his blanket over his head. Our conversation was clearly over.

'Thank you,' I said quietly to his enshrouded form and turned my attention back to the hills. On the slopes of our own mountain, a single bright spark danced above the drowning pool. I hadn't expected to hear good wishes from anyone, and it seemed to me like an omen. If it hadn't been for Hemmy's promise, I would have gone there and then.

CHAPTER SEVEN

When I went back to Hemmy's house the next morning the young chuffie was absent, presumably out on some errand or other. The old one was sprawled on the hearth-rug, all four legs splayed wide, utterly exhausted. Hemmy was sitting on a stool beside her, stirring a pot of peppernut porridge which gave off a strong, spicy smell. It wasn't one of my favourite foods, but I was hungry enough that morning to eat anything.

I made my way round the sleeping chuffie and gazed into the bubbling pot. The door was wide open and the fresh morning air circulated its optimism around the dark dome of the house. It was a day for setting out on an adventure, without a doubt.

'You've missed your start,' said Hemmy. 'The porters are already up in the hills and I just saw Simka go past with the goats.'

'Doesn't matter,' I said. 'I'm not going to see any beguilers by daylight, am I?'

'I suppose not,' said Hemmy, pouring porridge into two wooden bowls. I had been wondering how she filled her lonely days, but when I saw how slowly she did everything that particular mystery was solved. By the time she had finished clearing up after breakfast it would be time to start lunch. She handed me one of the bowls and put the other down beside her stool. Then she poured the last of yesterday's milk on to what was left in the pot and put it down beside the chuffie's nose. She prodded her with a stiff foot but she didn't stir.

'Poor old thing,' she said. 'She'll be leaving me soon, no doubt.'

She fell silent, and I realised that she would miss the old chuffie when it set out on its last journey. It was said in our village that chuffies went to the cloud mountain to die, but the truth was that it was a perpetual mystery. No one really knew where they came from or where they went when they were old and worn out, replete with the sorrows of our kind.

My thoughts were leading me into sadness, and the old creature stirred wearily in response. With an effort, I turned my mind to the future. As though she read my mind, Hemmy said, 'Maybe you think it's going to be simple. Just go and catch your beguiler, and that's it.'

I looked at her in bewilderment and realised that what she said was true. I expected to go up on to the mountain side as I had that other night and that would be it.

'If it was as easy as all that, though, why would everybody not do it?'

'Fear, I suppose. Fear that they might be led over the edge.'

'And don't you fear that?'

I began to feel a bit foolish. 'I hadn't thought that far,' I said. 'Do you think I really will catch one?'

'They say that it hasn't been done, don't they?' She picked up her porridge and began to eat it. I followed suit, half-heartedly, as she went on. 'But it isn't true. People have caught them. It's what happens afterwards that causes the problems.'

'What kind of problems?' I asked.

'From what I've heard,' she said indistinctly, through a gluey mouthful, 'it's easier to catch them, or at least to get hooked on to them, than it is to let them go.'

'If I caught one,' I said, sounding gluey myself, 'why should I want to let it go?'

She shrugged. Her bones creaked, or maybe it was the stool. 'If I was you,' she said, 'I wouldn't be in any rush to get myself entangled with one of those things. If I was you, I would do a bit of learning first.' The peppernut was burning my throat and making me cough and splutter, but it was one of the hazards of breakfast in our village at that time of year and I was quite used to it. I swallowed hard and wiped my watering eyes on my sleeve.

'What kind of learning?'

'Find out what happened to the others. That's what I would do.'

'Others?'

Hemmy said no more. She didn't need to. Despite my question, I knew exactly who she was talking about. The thought struck a chill into my heart and reminded me of the nature of the tradition which I had decided to follow. My first real doubts assailed me and my stomach contracted. I offered my remaining porridge to the old chuffie, but she still didn't stir.

When Hemmy had finished I took the bowls to the barrel outside the house and the neighbour's hens gathered round to see if there were any slops. As I washed up I could hear Hemmy groaning as she moved around the room. I left the bowls to dry on a rack in the sun and went back inside. There was a pot of water on the flue for tea, but Hemmy wasn't watching it. She was in the darkest corner of the room, beneath a window that was always, to my knowledge, shuttered, rummaging around in a wooden trunk. When she heard me come in she beckoned stiffly, without turning round.

Her back was bent double as she leaned over the chest. As I came up beside her, she pointed with a knobbly finger at a piece of folded material.

'Take it out,' she said.

I picked it up. It was a large shawl or a small blanket, I'm not sure which, made of cotton. It had been dyed, like many of the clothes in the village, with the yellowish clay that the weavers dig from a muddy hollow beneath the furthest terraces. It's one of the cheapest dyes, used for work clothes and bedding. The brighter and more delicate colours come from berries and flowers and they take a lot of labour to gather.

The shawl, blanket, whatever it was, disappointed me. I had expected Hemmy to produce some sort of magical items which would help me on the adventure, but I couldn't see what use that grubby old thing would be.

'It doesn't look much,' she said, 'but you'll wonder how you ever lived without it when you come to use it.'

'Why?' I said.

'I have no idea. But the person who gave it to me told me that and I have no reason to doubt him.'

'Who was that?'

Hemmy looked at me sideways as though wondering whether I could be trusted. Finally she said, almost like an admission, 'Dabbo.'

I had succeeded in keeping his name out of my mind, but it seemed that I was going to have to think about him. He was legendary, the madman of the village. Even though I didn't remember him at all, I felt that I knew him. Everyone in the village had stories about him. He wouldn't talk to people, they said, only to chuffies and goats, with whom he preferred to live. He spent most of each year in some hermit hut up on the mountain and only came down, dirty and ragged, when the weather was too bad for him to survive up there. Then he would refuse to go into any house but stay outside with the yard chuffies. People said that he used to spend hours at night staring up at the mountainside, even in blizzards, and sometimes he keened or whined to himself and all the chuffies of the village couldn't comfort him. He was harmless to others but a torment, it seemed, to himself. And he was, of course, a beguiler-hunter.

'He left these things with me before he died,' said Hemmy, looking back into the trunk. She pointed to a little coil of gut and I picked it up.

'Is it for catching them?' I asked.

Hemmy snorted as if I had said something foolish. 'Don't you know that there's no rope in the world will hold a beguiler?'

I nodded, slightly embarrassed.

'No,' she went on. 'This is to hold you. To catch yourself. Whenever you're on the track of a beguiler and you find yourself in a dangerous place, tie one end of this to your ankle and the other end to a tree.'

'That?' I said. 'But that would never take my weight!'

'Leave it, then.'

I looked at the coiled-up string and knew that whatever I thought about it I wouldn't leave it. I wrapped the corner of the yellow shawl around it and tied a knot, which seemed to satisfy Hemmy. But she was not finished yet. She stooped still further into the trunk, pulled out a sheaf of stiff, woolly-edged papers, and handed them to me.

I leafed through them. They were drawings, made in charcoal and green grub-wood ink. Most of them just seemed to be scribbles; dots and spirals and pairs of wild-looking eyes, floating in mid-air, like the crude scratchings that small children make. Only one of them resembled anything real. It was of a small, stone building with a flag-stone roof, standing on the brow of a hill. The detail was perfect, and it was hard to believe that it was drawn by the same hand that had produced the other chaotic sketches.

'Did Dabbo draw these?' I asked.

'Hmm.' Hemmy was still rummaging around in the bottom of the trunk, and at last she found what she was looking for. In her hand was a small leather bag like a coin purse. She rattled it and it made a sound like peppernuts knocking together.

I reached out for it, but she moved her hand away from me, behind her.

'Not so fast. Can you follow orders?'

'Orders?' I said. 'Whose orders?'

'Anyone's orders. Life's orders?'

I was about to say that of course I could follow orders when some more honest inner voice intervened. It was not true. Following orders was one thing that I was particularly bad at. I regularly failed to succeed in my Intentions and resolutions which were, I supposed, my own orders. When it came to the things that other people asked me to do I had a strange attitude. My first reaction was always to feel indignant and refuse. Following that would be a reversal; I would feel guilty and bend over backwards to accommodate the person who had asked me the favour, but it was often too late. And as for life's orders, that was self-explanatory. Would I be going off hunting for beguilers if I was a natural follower of life's rules and regulations?

Hemmy let my silence run on until the answer to her question was obvious. Then she said, 'Nor could Dabbo.'

I said nothing, looked at the wild drawings in my hand, thinking about how he ended up. After a while Hemmy went on, 'He was a bit like you in some ways. Dithered about his Great Intention until he was nineteen, then went out into the were-woods and killed a snowbuck, to prove that he could. Although he hadn't yet made a Great Intention, he was nevertheless a man. A year or so later he announced that he was going after beguilers and was gone from the village for more than twenty years.'

'Twenty years!'

'Yes. We all assumed that he was dead, but one night in autumn as the snows were beginning he came back. He was as thin as a broom handle; even the lice had abandoned ship, I think. My husband, Bream, had been killed in a landslide the year before, and since that left me with plenty of space and no responsibilities it was natural that I should take Dabbo in. No one expected him to survive, but he did, and as soon as the snows melted in the spring he set off again up the mountain. That became his pattern after that, to come back to the village during the worst of the snows and leave again after the thaw. He wouldn't stay in my house the next winter and never did again, but we had become friends of a sort and he would visit me quite often.'

The water in the pot began to steam and Hemmy, who had been slowly straightening up as she told her story, now moved around the wall of the room towards the fire. She didn't speak again until she had come to a halt and balanced herself. Then she continued.

'Dabbo used to wear out chuffies like no one I've ever met. Even worse than me, he was.'

I looked at the exhausted creature on the floor and wondered how much longer she would stay. Hemmy had, indeed, had quite a succession of chuffies.

'It's just as well there's no shortage of them,' she went on. 'Otherwise the village might have had to take action.'

She threw a small handful of eazle-corns into the boiling water and then began to crumble dried puffberries. It was one of my favourite brews. I shaved the sugar for her, then we sat back and waited for everything to infuse.

'Where was I?' said Hemmy. 'Oh, yes. Dabbo. As I was saying, he used to come and visit me quite often. His mood was very changeable. Sometimes he would sit perfectly quietly, and at those times there was no point in talking to him because it was clear that he wasn't taking in anything that you were saying. Then, at other times, he chattered non-stop. I don't know how much of what he said was real and how much of it was made up, but it was during those times that he told me about some of his exploits with the beguilers and about these things that he had.' She nodded towards the articles which I was holding in my lap. 'He used to leave them with me when he was down in the village and collect them again when he went off in the spring. They were the sum of his possessions and they never changed. He was here in the village when he died, which is how I come to have his things. I've had them now for thirteen years, wondering what to do with them. That was why, when you announced your Intention last evening I quickly revised my own.' She smiled, rustily. 'I was going to say the same thing again.'

I laughed, struck by the absurdity of it. 'You may be well prepared for your death by now, Hemmy, but I don't think your death wants you.'

She nodded, the smile still on her face. I dropped the drawings back into the trunk and poured out the brew. I tried to wake the chuffie for her share but she was still a long way from morning.

'You haven't told me what it was you meant when you asked me if I could follow orders,' I said.

Hemmy slurped her drink. 'What Dabbo told me, or what I managed to gather from his rantings, is this. The shawl will never let the cold into you. The coil of gut will never be too short and it will never break. Those things are easy, he said. But what is not easy is the rule of the beguilers' eyes.'

'The what?'

'That's what fills the little bag, so he told me.'

'Beguilers' eyes?' I said, with ridicule in my voice. I began to tug at the knot which secured the top of the bag but Hemmy said, with more urgency than I would have believed possible. 'No, no! Whatever else you do, you must never open the bag unless you need to. That is the rule, the order that you must be sure that you can follow. Never open the bag unless you need to. Can you stick to that?'

It seemed absurd to me. 'Why shouldn't I?'

'I don't know,' said Hemmy. 'But Dabbo couldn't. That's what made him mad.'

A chill ran through my bones. 'How do you know?'

'He told me so. Or at least, I gathered it from some of the things he said. The first year he was back. He warned me about the bag.'

It was easier to be sceptical. 'Maybe he was mad anyway?' I said.

'Maybe,' said Hemmy. She finished the rest of her drink and then said, 'Maybe you are, too.'

The chuffie groaned, disturbed by the changing emotions running through the room. I did my best to control my feelings. The poor creature had enough on her plate as it was.

As calmly as I could I finished my drink. Then I tied the little bag into another corner of the shawl, which I folded and laid across my shoulder.

'What else should I take with me?' I asked Hemmy.

The old woman shrugged. 'It's up to you,' she said. 'But remember. On this kind of journey you can never travel too light.'

PART TWO

CHAPTER EİGHT

My way out of the village led past my house. No one was there, so I slipped in and went to the room I shared with Lenko. I was shocked to discover that all my things had already been cleared out, and for a long time I stood staring at my empty corner, unwilling to believe what I was seeing.

Until then, I suppose that it had all seemed like a game; a test perhaps, of myself and my parents. But now I knew that it was real. I had offered my Intention and separated myself from the family. They had, according to their duties under the Given Law, already removed all reminders of me from their sight. Whether they liked it or not, as far as they were concerned, I no longer existed.

My despair drew Tigo in from the yard. He snuffled around at my face and tried to wrap himself around my legs.

'It's all right, Tigo,' I said. 'I can handle it.'

'Wopplecryst?' he said.

I nodded, numbly. 'I'm going,' I said. 'I just wanted to collect some things.'

He helped me search until we found my belongings, stuffed into two cloth bags in the winter coat-room. At least they were still in the house and the discovery lit a glimmer of hope in my heart. Despite the Law, some small corner of my parents' lives still had room for me. Perhaps this separation was as difficult for them as it was for me? The priests could regulate their actions, after all, but not their feelings.

I emptied everything out and sorted through it, hampered continually by Tigo's desperate efforts to cheer me up. I chose warm clothes and precious bits and pieces and put them into one of the bags. But as soon as I hefted it on to my shoulder, I knew I had chosen too much. I emptied the bag again and, after a long deliberation, decided that Hemmy had been right. I needed to travel light. I was starting a new life and couldn't afford to encumber myself with the trappings of the old one. When I left the house, I was wearing my winter boots instead of my sandals, and my filled water-skin was slung over my shoulder. All the other things, even my snowbuck jacket, were back in the bags where I had found them.

The boots looked and felt ridiculous as I walked through the hot, dusty streets of the village. But I soon realised that it didn't matter. As far as my community was concerned, I wasn't even there. No one looked at me at all. I could have been wearing a pair of antlers and a tail; it wouldn't have made any difference.

I couldn't leave the village fast enough, but as I walked along the path which led to the hill-side I was plagued by reminders of all the things that I had grown accustomed to having at home, and needing. I had no food, no spare clothes, no bed-roll. I had no matches to light a fire and no pot to heat water in even if I'd had food to cook in it. Before I was out of sight of the village I was, despite the fur-lined boots, beginning to get cold feet. Very cold indeed.

I might have turned back if there had been anywhere to go. My heart was still heavy with the memory of what I had found at home, and I didn't need any further confirmation of my ostracised condition. But I was about to get it, anyway.

Ahead of me on the path, coming in the opposite direction, was a small group of women who were bringing head-loads of firewood down from the trees. On another morning I might have been among them, bringing an extra load for one of the elders who couldn't fetch it for himself. But today I was very much alone. I moved off the track on to the bank as they passed by, and not one of them greeted me or acknowledged that I was there. Not even the woman who was bringing up the rear. My mother.

Her eyes were cast down and her expression was hard and inscrutable. My heart went out to her, imagining her pain at having to deny me. But what I saw next changed my feelings abruptly.

A young chuffie bumbled along at her heels, full of enthusiasm and, quite clearly, bursting with pride at its new appointment. I was unprepared for the shock that its appearance created in me. Perhaps I was wrong about my parents' sentiments. Perhaps they were only too pleased to be rid of me. Now, at least, our family could be like the others in the village.

I walked on again, trying to pretend that I didn't care. But I did. The incident had been painful, but worse than that, it had made me aware of how utterly alone I was.

I saw a few other people as I climbed; some of the men and boys harvesting timber in the forest, a group of girls gathering twine-cane for making chairs and a couple of smaller boys cutting eazle-wood. I went over to them to ask for a piece because my teeth felt furry after the sweet tea, but they ran off, giggling. That made me angry. If I wasn't mad yesterday, how could I be mad today? It made me want to prove to them all that what I was doing was as valid and purposeful as the way they had chosen to spend their lives, and for a while I strode on with renewed resolve.

But it didn't last long. An hour or so later, the sun was reaching its highest point and even among the bushes where I sat down to rest it was too hot for comfort. Down in the village the smaller children would be swimming in the pond while the adults slept or gathered in the cool tea-shops to chat away the worst of the afternoon heat. The leaves around me were wilting slightly, as they did every afternoon, and I was wilting, too.

Because of the way our 'lap' juts out of the steep mountainside, the streams that run down from the melting snows pass to either side of our hill. The village was built there because when the spring floods are at their worst, the streams and rivers swell so much that they sweep away any terraces that are built closer to them. But it means also that if it weren't for the drowning pool we would have famished from drought during the recent long spell of hot, dry summers.

Further up the mountain and further down it there are streams where I could have dangled my feet and refreshed myself. But here, above the village, they were all dry. Even the birds were quiet; even the insects were idling in the heat. The best I could do was to fold the yellow shawl beneath my head and try to rest.

As I drowsed, the sun disappeared behind the peaks. Strictly speaking it had gone down, but the horizon is so high here that there is still another two or three hours of daylight after the sun has vanished. I spent the first hour putting more distance between myself and the village, knowing that the further I got from it the more chance I would have of finding wild food. When I thought I had walked far enough I settled down to some foraging, finding eazle first to clean my teeth and then, by following a young wing-tail, two fistfuls of ground-plums, as rich and nutritious as good cheese. Food never tasted so good and I didn't regret at all that I had no brew to wash them down. A few minutes later I came across a wild whisker-tree and I picked about two dozen of the spidery fruit, even though I wasn't hungry at all by then. I found a clearing in the bushes and laid out my shawl on top of the crisp grass. Then I spread out the whisker-fruit to begin drying. They would make a useful reserve if fresh food became scarce.

As the light reddened in the west and began to depart, the birds and insects became suddenly frantic, as though they too had been drowsing in the sun and now had to make up for a wasted day. I wrapped my fruit in my shawl and quietly followed a pair of tracker-birds who were fetching orange bramberries for their raucous children. It's always a difficult decision, whether or not to bother with bramberries. Their leaves are covered with a kind of hair which has barbs on the end. If you catch your clothes on them it can take half an hour to disentangle yourself, and they can, if you are very unfortunate, even grab your bare skin. And after all that trouble, they're not that nice; not as nice as puffberries or yellowpips.

I rolled up my sleeves and gathered a few mouthfuls. The way things were, I decided that I couldn't really afford to waste any opportunity to eat even if I wasn't hungry. By the time I had finished it was nearly dark, so I went back the way I had come and began to descend from the forest towards the drowning-pool.

I was so sure that they would be there, the same beguilers that I had seen the last time. I followed the route that they had led me on before and settled myself on the northern lip of the high bank, far from the byre where the men and oxen were already shut away from the coming night. Feeling slightly foolish, even though there was no one around to see me, I followed mad Dabbo's instructions and tied one end of the gut coil to a young flossy oak tree and the other end to my ankle. The heat showed no sign of diminishing even though it was dark, so I sat on the cotton shawl instead of wrapping it round me. Cross-legged, hugging my knees in anticipation, I waited.

Behind me, at the edge of the forest, a nightangel was singing. It went through an extraordinary repertoire of sounds, from plaintive sobbing to sparkling chickering to melodic passages that stunned me with their simple beauty. I sank deep into its changing moods and came to the realisation that if I was that bird, or the mate that it was wooing, I would truly understand what love was. Not like the chuffie-coloured love that bore the name among the people of my village, but the real thing; so much more mysterious and profound. I didn't know if it was possible for humans to experience it. It seemed doubtful, somehow, especially for someone as isolated and detached as I was.

In the end I nodded off, still sitting there with my cheek resting on my scrunched-up knees, still listening to the nightangel. When I woke it was cold and I felt as stiff as old Hemmy. It took me ten minutes to unfold my legs and get the circulation going in them again, but after that I felt better and quite enjoyed the freshness of the pre-dawn air.

I was surprised and pleased to find that I had no fear of the darkness. On the contrary, I delighted in it as though it was something that I had been unjustly denied throughout the whole of my life. The moon was only just past full, of course, and I knew that there would be much darker nights to come, but I felt, nonetheless, as I kept my watch that I had passed some kind of test.

There were still no beguilers, though, and the morning came without bringing them to me. I remembered the night that they had danced before my eyes and wished that I had taken the opportunity then to try and catch one. Could I have done it? And if so, how?

I remembered Hemmy saying that it had been done. Perhaps she was right. Perhaps I would have to follow in the footsteps of those who had gone before me, if only to avoid making the same mistakes as they had. I got up and made my way up the mountainside before the men emerged from the byre to get the oxen ready for drawing water.

But I didn't enjoy the spectacular dawn. The prospect of meeting with the legendary Shirsha filled me with apprehension. I would have to find out for myself whether she was mad or not. If she was, then I would learn what madness was and know if I suffered from it myself. If she wasn't, if she was just a searcher like myself, then she might, as Hemmy had suggested, have something to teach me.

CHAPTER NINE

With the sun came the heat, and the whisker-fruit that I had wrapped in my shawl were surprisingly heavy. Walking up the steep hill-sides was nothing new to me; I often came up here, collecting firewood or wild food. Even so I found the morning's walk hard going.

It would have been easier if I could have stayed on the main porters' tracks, or even on the smaller paths made by foresters and herders, but I was too wary about being seen to risk them. I had no desire to encounter my mother again, or any of the other villagers. So I kept close to the tracks but not on them, and every few minutes I stopped to rest and listen carefully to the sounds of the forest all around.

They gave me clues to what was going on. Quite often when the birds and beasts were silent it was only because of my presence, but I came to learn that if I stayed still for a certain length of time they would forget me and carry on about their business. But if that time elapsed and they were still silent it meant there was something or someone else around apart from me; when that happened I found myself a quiet corner and waited until I heard the intruder pass or until the forest sounds returned and told me that all was well.

It happened rarely, though, and I made quite good progress that morning. When the heat reached its worst I began to look around for a cool place to rest. There was no sign of a stream, but when I was about ready to drop I found a marshy spot where an underground spring trickled to the surface, and I lay at its edge and dozed with the cool dampness seeping through my clothes.

I didn't move again until I heard the life of the forest winding down towards the end of the day. I filled up my water-skin and set out in search of food, but although I spent quite some time digging for ground-plums, all I got for my pains was dirty hands and I had to fall back on my dried rations.

I ate as I walked, eager to get some distance behind me before nightfall. What I planned was to find an open patch of ground where I could watch for beguilers in the dark, so I left the path and headed directly up-hill through the trees. But as dusk began to fall, and then more solid darkness, I had still not found a way out into the open and when it became too dark to see any further I had to make my bed where I found myself, among the trees.

It wasn't pleasant in there. It was quite different from the hill-side above the drowning-pool which was open to the moon and the stars. Here the trees and bushes closed over me; I could see almost nothing, and since I had arrived in total darkness I had no clear idea of where I was or what my surroundings looked like. The rustlings of the nocturnal creatures seemed ominously loud and close and I rolled my bundle of provisions up into a ball and put them beneath my head as a pillow. It seemed to me that I stayed awake for all eternity, listening to my surroundings and trying not to let my imagination run away with me again, but I may have slept. Either that or my thoughts ran into dreams without my noticing. In any case I woke, or became alert, not knowing whether the sound I heard came from outside my head or inside it.

It was a long, terrible shriek, full of longing and pain. I opened my eyes wide and stared at the darkness, waiting. It didn't come again. With only the memory, the dream memory of it, I couldn't judge accurately which direction the sound had come from or whether it was near or distant. At times my recollection was that it was enormously loud and clear. At other times I thought that it had been distant and faint. But every time I tried to sleep again it returned to my mind, a long, hollow moan, which made my heart pound and my eyes snap open to search the darkness.

There was no doubt that the sound was the cry of a beguiler, but there was something different about it that made it far more alarming than any I had heard before. It evoked no desire in me to get up and pursue it. Instead it made me fearful; it made me want to hide from it in the way the villagers hid from the beguilers who called in the streets. As I lay there in utter loneliness, I began to believe that I hadn't heard the sound at all but that it had come from deep within my own soul, the proof of a madness which might not have emerged yet but was beginning to awaken and give itself expression. I was no longer so enamoured of the darkness. It seemed to live and breathe all around me as though it had a will and substance of its own. At home in my parents' house, where I never had the need to reach for them, were leaf-lanterns and butter lamps. Here there was no way to find light. None at all. There was nothing for me to do except wait.

By the time morning came I was close to hopelessness. My body was stiff and sore from the tense and restless night and my mind was exhausted, numbed by the continual passage of fearful thoughts which had flowed like hot fluid through my brain. But nocturnal terrors lose their force when daylight comes. Just as it is impossible to imagine the cold of winter while the sun is roasting your skin, so it is impossible to remember the fear of nightmares when the morning comes and the world appears before you in the same form that it always has.

I was quite high on the mountain by now, about halfway between the village and the snow-line. The altitude I had gained the previous day made a difference to the temperature and it was not uncomfortable. The woods were full of chattering and fluttering life, and I was so engrossed by the behaviour of the birds and beasts that I covered miles without realising it.

A yellow-pip grove brought me to a halt. The berries were smaller at the higher altitude, but they were firmer, too, and tasted more substantial. When I had eaten as much as I could and wrapped another meal of them in a free corner of the shawl, I carried on up the hill-side. As I got higher the vegetation began to change. The trees there were smaller and clearly had to struggle harder for existence than their cousins further down. There were no planks to be made from these crooked and stunted trunks, and if it wasn't for the rare delicacies that were sometimes to be found at such heights, no members of our community would ever venture up so high.

As the day progressed the hard-wood trees gave way to rhododendron, not flowering yet but showing the first signs of making buds. In past years I had been up there during the season when their blossoms covered the whole mountain with pinks and purples and whites, but now the trees were dreary and dark. I kept a close look-out for snow-apples, which are quite common up there, but I didn't find any.

I found something better, though. Pushing its perpendicular branches out strongly, so that the rhododendrons on either side had to lean away to find light, was one of the finest jub trees that I had ever seen. I was perplexed at first because the branches were laden with ripe nuts as big as my fist, and I couldn't understand how it was that they hadn't been harvested yet. I was debating with my conscience about whether or not I could steal a few when it began to dawn on me that the tree had no name inscribed upon it. Three times I circled round it, inspecting the trunk from top to bottom. I was right; there was no name.

It was an extraordinary discovery. Finding an unowned jub tree is about as likely as finding a gold mine, and nearly as valuable. I shinned up the tree and knocked down a dozen of them. Most of them I added to the weighty load in my shawl, but I kept out a couple of small ones to eat before I moved on. I had never tasted one before, but I had heard that there's nothing like a jub-nut if you're hungry. They have a wonderful invigorating quality, like eating condensed sunshine, which is why they're so valuable. People buy them for sickly children or convalescents. Apothecaries grind them up and add them to tonics or aphrodisiac potions for the wealthy. The two that I ate sent my spirits soaring and filled me with energy for the next leg of the journey, so that despite the considerable extra weight I covered a lot of ground during the next couple of hours.

In the cool of the early evening I came to a small clearing which caught the yellow light of the setting sun. Looking back later, I realised that I should have stayed in that pleasant spot and made an early camp for the night, but I was not adept at following life's orders and I soon got up and pushed on. I pushed on so hard that I came out of the rhododendron belt and into the druze bushes just as it was growing dark, and as I searched for a place to sleep I wished that I had been in less of a hurry.

No one ever spends time in the were-forest unless they have to. The black leaves of the druze bushes lower the spirits as well as being highly poisonous. It's considered a dangerous weed, partly because the plants store a huge amount of water in their roots and leaves, and if they become too plentiful in an area they can take water from the ground that would otherwise trickle down to the levels where we grow our food. If it were allowed to, it would spread down the mountainside towards the plain, but one of the main duties of a forester is to cut back any druze that shows up among the trees. The rhododendron seems to be a good match for it and provides a natural barrier, but occasionally a strong out-growth will break through and begin to spread. If that happens a party from the village goes up to clear it out, but there's no point in trying to plant anything else in its place because the soil where it grows is poisoned for years after it has been cut. So the area has to be checked out on a regular basis unless the druze grows back and re-establishes itself.

I back-tracked for a few minutes, but in the dusk I must have been travelling among a mixture of druze and rhododendron for some time without realising it and there was no sign of an end to it as I descended. Darkness was catching up with me, and in desperation I made for a heavy thicket of rhododendron which I hoped would be untainted by druze. It isn't that contact with it will harm you, not in the short term anyway. But it's difficult to describe the effect that those black leaves have upon the mind. Not only do they lack colour themselves, but they seem to draw all other colours out of their environment so the world appears to consist of nothing except black and grey. I didn't want to wake up to that.

It wasn't until I stopped walking that I realised how cold it had become. I was only a mile or two below the permanent snow-line now, and the air smelled of ice already and held its crisp breath. I unpacked the food from my shawl before I cooled down too much and wrapped it around me to keep the heat in. My supplies tumbled around my feet and I laid out a mat of rhododendron leaves and heaped everything on to it, picking out the yellow-pips and eating them as I went along. I knew that snatchers didn't come as high as this, but I wasn't sure about pig-rats. There was no way to be sure they wouldn't rob me. The best I could do was to curl myself up around my pile of food and hope for the best.

By now it was fully dark, but although I was physically tired I was far from sleep. I lay and listened to the last birds settling themselves in for the night and tried to ignore the depth of the silence that lay behind their rustlings. I was comfortable where I lay, and the shawl was surprisingly warm, but I feared the vast, empty silence of the mountain above. I longed for the comforting sound of the nightangel's song, but I knew there was no chance of hearing it up there in the druze. So I tried to remember it instead, and at last I began to drift towards sleep.

CHAPTER TEN

The sound, when it came again, cut through me like an ice-cold dagger. All the warmth that I had preserved inside my shawl seemed to depart in that instant. This time there was no mistaking that it was real and that it came from somewhere out there in the night and not from inside my mind. The sound was anguished, agonized, ripping through the night like desperate claws, grasping at my soul.

I stayed dead still, clutching at the edge of the yellow shawl the way a baby grips her mother's collar, grasping for comfort. My heart was hammering wildly in my chest, urging me to run; to put the source of such fear as far behind me as possible.

But I couldn't run. Some sense of pride, or of purpose, or both, was holding me firm against my fear. And there was another thing as well; less clear to me but no less powerful. The beguiler's cry sent shock and terror lancing through my heart, but those weren't the only feelings it evoked. As though it were barbed, the sound had planted hooks in me and my desire was divided between advancing and retreating.

For a while longer I was held in a stalemate, paralysed by indecision. Then, almost before I knew it, I found myself getting to my feet.

The beguiler was silent now, but its whereabouts was clear to me as I made my way through the druze. I walked uphill and to my left, angling away from the porters' trail and towards the unscaled peak of the Great Mother. There was still no light, but there were varying shades of darkness as I moved through the night. The druze bushes crouched like malevolent beasts and seemed to bar every route I tried to take. I had to back-track constantly and make winding detours, but the long-gone sound of the beguiler had etched its point of origin clearly on to my mind, and I never lost my sense of direction. I was in a black maze in the black night, and so intent upon finding my way through it that I lost all sense of why I was there or what I would do if and when I found my way out.

My journey ended abruptly. One minute I was fighting my way through the druze and the next I was clear of it, standing on the edge of a wide clearing and looking up at a sandstone cliff which reared up above me until it vanished into the darkness.

Through a gap in the clouds I glimpsed a half moon, lying on her back as though she had fallen. Her dim light shone upon the cliff face and suddenly I knew where I was. The whole face of the crag was pocked by holes and laced with hand-carved paths. I had arrived at the lepers' caves.

There were no longer any lepers there, I knew. There hadn't been for several generations. As I looked up at the cliff I remembered hearing that the strange formation had been made by water forcing its way through the stone, and although the melting snows had now found another route to bring them down the mountainside, there were times during the year when the caves were practically uninhabitable because of the damp. I had learnt that because it was a story regularly told to the children in the village; how the lepers had come down from their caves looking for shelter one year and the elders had been thrown into a quandary about them. It would go against the principles of the village to refuse hospitality, yet it would endanger the population to have the lepers living among the people. In the end they had brought the outcasts to the buzz-bat cave, a huge cavern which lies about a mile below the village. A strong stream runs through the middle of it, but it never bursts its banks and the lepers were dry and happy there until the weather changed and their own homes dried out. After that they came every wet season and set up camp there, sharing quite happily with the buzz-bats, until Bodwa the World-Widener, the best of all the Law-Givers, had condemned their enforced exile and built them a city of their own on the plains. She had been the one who allowed men to enter the priesthood, and opened the trading paths between the divided mountain fiefdoms, and permitted inter-marriage between the closed clans. She had been dead for more than a hundred years, but her likeness hung above every hearth in every village in the land and she would never be forgotten.

I took a step forward into the clearing and at the same moment I saw the beguiler. It darted out of one of the caves, about mid-way up the cliff and hung in the air, high above my head. From that distance it appeared tiny to me, but even so I found that I could clearly see the golden eyes, which met my gaze full on, and held it. I was fleetingly aware of that sense of recognition, as though I had always known the being that hovered there before me. But before I could follow my thoughts, the sensation was gone. The expression in the beguiler's eyes revealed a ferocious, jealous love, and it produced the same emotion in my heart. Then it disappeared, back into the dark interior.

It had only been outside the cave for an instant, but its effect on me in that brief space of time had been profound. I was like a fish on a line, but a willing one, all too ready to be reeled in by the beguiler's possessive power. Every emotion that I had ever experienced seemed to ignite in me at once. I burned with joy and sorrow and envy; with longing and fear and revulsion. For a moment I tried to resist what was happening to me, but the connection stretched my heart too hard and I found myself moving forwards, drawn by some will that was no longer my own.

I crossed the clearing, vaguely aware of leaving darkness behind me and heading towards some new and glorious light. I kept my gaze fixed upon the point where I had seen the beguiler, and before I knew it I was at the foot of the cliff, craning my neck to keep the mouth of the cave within my view.

I ought to have realised the truth of the situation as soon as I became aware of the rope guide-rail. It ran up the cliff, zigzagging along the interwoven paths, leading from where I stood right up to the cave from which the beguiler had emerged. But it was a sign of how mesmerised I was that it seemed entirely appropriate to me that I should be given any assistance I needed, whether natural or supernatural, to enable me to reach my shining goal.

With one hand I held my shawl around me, and with the other I gripped the rope. It was pegged into the sandstone at regular intervals with stout wooden wedges, and although it had been worn smooth by use, it was firmly fixed and had no slack anywhere along its length.

I was glad of it. The paths were narrow and were so badly worn in places that it would have been impossible to pass along them without the hand-rail. Going up towards the cave was easy, but now and then the rope angled away, causing me to turn my back on the cave and the beguiler inside. Every time that happened I became acutely distressed and had to drag myself along those short stretches, breaking out into anxious, clammy sweats.

Not even the smallest part of my mind was free from the beguiler's influence. I had no awareness, none whatsoever, of the danger I was walking myself into. As I climbed the last stretch of the path, the only thought in my mind was of the shining reward that awaited me. I stepped on to the broad ledge outside the cave mouth and didn't even pause before bending my head and ducking through the low entrance.

I saw the beguiler, hovering in the deep darkness, some distance away. Then there was a flurry of violent movement beside me and, before I had a chance to react, everything went black.

CHAPTER ELEVEN

For several, terrifying moments I had absolutely no idea what was happening. Something was covering my head, I was falling to the floor, and there was laboured breathing in the air around me. I was trying to strike out at my unseen assailant, but my arms weren't responding to my instructions.

Then everything became clear to me. Someone had thrown a heavy blanket over my head, knocked me to the ground and wrapped a tight rope around me, pinning my arms to my sides. In the same moment, I knew who it was and I understood, too late, all the warning signs that I ought to have heeded. I even knew why Shirsha had caught me and trussed me up like this. The beguiler I had seen was hers, and she was protecting it. The shock had broken the powerful link between it and me and brought me back to my senses.

'I'm sorry,' I babbled to the unseen Shirsha. 'I'll go away, I won't bother you again if you let me go.'

Shirsha didn't answer, but I could hear her panting after her exertions. She was close to me; very close. Leaning over me, perhaps. I envisioned a weapon in her hands; a heavy club, already raised and about to descend upon my skull.

'Please don't hurt me,' I pleaded. 'Please let me go.'

Her breathing began to return to normal and I heard her moving away from me. Not far, but out of reach. My shoulder was jammed against one of the walls and I slowly wriggled my way into a sitting position. The rope around me was too tight. It pinched my arms and I could already feel my hands beginning to go tingly from lack of circulation. I tried to shift them a bit, slowly and carefully so it wouldn't look as if I was trying to escape.

'Why did you come here?'

Shirsha's voice was not at all as I had expected. I had thought she would be older; frail as Hemmy, and that her madness would be apparent when she spoke. But this voice was as firm and as strong as the arms that had so easily subdued me, and my preconceived image of its owner was changing rapidly. I was no less afraid, though. Her tone was prickly and defensive. I was not out of danger yet.

I didn't know how to answer. I wanted to reassure her; I couldn't possibly tell her that I had been drawn here by her precious beguiler. But she knew.

'It brung you here, didn't it?'

'I didn't know it was yours,' I said. 'I'm sorry. I wouldn't have come if I did.'

She paused, unsure what to make of my answer, and then she said, 'What were you doing on my mountain?'

I searched for a suitable lie but my wits seemed to have deserted me. There was nothing for it but to come clean.

'I was looking for you, Shirsha.'

'For me? Why? No one comes near me. What do you want with me?'

She sounded threatened and I prayed that I hadn't said the wrong thing.

'I wanted to learn from you,' I said.

'Learn what?' she snapped.

'What you know. About the beguilers. I . . .'

In the pause that followed I could hear her breath hissing in and out between her teeth, as though she was cold, or afraid, or both. I was a bit cold myself. During the struggle my shawl had slipped from my shoulders and was now scrumpled up around my waist.

'I didn't mean to follow your beguiler,' I said at last. 'I didn't know it was yours.'

Shirsha still said nothing and I babbled on because her silence scared me. 'I made a Great Intention. To catch . . .'

'You're one of them,' she said. 'I knew one of them would come snooping around some time. But you're not having it, you hear me?'

'I don't want it,' I said, and I could hear my own muffled desperation inside the blanket. The air was stale in there, and smelled of damp and mould. 'Just let me go and I'll leave you alone. I'll never come back, I promise.'

Shirsha gave no sign that she had heard me. 'It called you, didn't it? It came looking for you?'

'It . . . It mightn't have been looking for me. I just saw it.'

'It doesn't want me no more,' said Shirsha. 'It knows it can't win, see?'

'Win?'

'It wants my soul and then it would be free, but I won't give it. No. That would be the end.'

For the first time I detected a hint of vulnerability in her tone, and I answered instinctively. 'Then why do you stay here?'

'What else can I do?' I couldn't see her, but I sensed her turning away from me in the darkness and I was aware of the beguiler's power in the air of the cave. 'There is nothing so beautiful in all the world, and it is mine. How can I give it up?'

It would not have occurred to me before to defend village life, but here in the damp cave, with the high altitude cold soaking into my bones, it seemed to have many attractions.

'But don't you miss the village, Shirsha?' I said. 'Don't you miss warmth and comfort and security?'

'Bah,' she said. 'Warmth, security. There is more warmth

and security on the cloud mountain than there is in your precious village. I miss nothing.' By the tone of her voice I knew it was true.

'Perhaps life disappointed you in some way?'

'Life, people, it's all a disappointment. If it wasn't, why would you be here?'

'To see what more there might be, I suppose.' It occurred to me as I was saying it that perhaps life held disappointments for everyone, and the only thing that made people like Shirsha and I different was that we were unable to accept those disappointments and carry on. But here there was merely more disillusionment. Shirsha had found her beguiler and, in some way, caught it. But her life seemed drab and empty, even worse than life in the village. 'Will you stay here forever, then?' I asked.

'Why should I want to go anywhere else? I have all I need.'

I had only been on the mountainside for a few days, but it was already clear to me that, with a certain amount of work and forward thinking, it would be quite possible to live off the wild foods which were to be found up there. In one sense it was probably true that Shirsha had all she needed, but the tone of her voice suggested otherwise. It suggested that although she had food, and a home, and the beguiler that she had sought after, her heart was empty.

'Where did you find it, Shirsha?' I asked. 'If you tell me I'll go away. I'll go and I won't look back. I promise. I'll get one of my own.'

'Then you'll have to go where Dabbo went.'

The sound of his name shocked me. I wondered if Shirsha was aware that I had his shawl, that the few clues he had left were all I had to go on.

'He brought it out. Out of the cloud mountain. But it wanted me, see? It wanted me, and Dabbo couldn't do a thing about it. He used to come around here with his whimpering and wailing, trying to get it back. But it wouldn't leave me for him. Go back, I told him. Go and get another one. But he was gutless, see? Didn't dare go in again.'

My heart sank. 'The cloud mountain? Will I have to go there?'

'Did you not know that? Did you come hunting for a beguiler and not know that you would have to visit the cloud mountain?'

'How should I know that? If beguilers take travellers from the paths, why shouldn't one come to me? I'm a traveller, after all.'

'You're softer than me, child,' said Shirsha. 'That's why it tried to get away from me and come to you. But you're still tougher than most. They don't like us the same way they like those others, those villagers down there, all puffed up with chuffie love. They're the ones they want. They're the easy ones. You could wander the mountain paths for twenty years and never get close to another beguiler.'

I fell silent, pondering this new development. There was no way of knowing how far away the cloud mountain was, or even what it was. Some said there was land beneath the ever-present mists; others said there wasn't. The common belief was that chuffies went there to die, but I had always thought this was just an easy excuse to cover the mystery of their sudden disappearances. I sighed and thought of my jub trees growing a few miles away. That sort of life would be so much easier.

I was no longer afraid. It was horrible being trussed up like that, but all my instincts were telling me that Shirsha would do me no harm. She seemed to be sunk in thought. In the heavy silence, I realised that there was a discrepancy between what I had learnt about beguilers and what was happening here. When I was under the spell of Shirsha's beguiler, I was sure it could have led me anywhere, but Shirsha was still here, after all those years.

'How can you live with it?' I asked. 'And how is it that you can look at it so easily and not be drawn in?'

The silence that followed was long and cold. I wondered if I had said the wrong thing. I thought of the other things Dabbo had left with Hemmy. Maybe I could use the beguilers' eyes to get myself out of this hole? I tried to inch the edge of the shawl through my fingers, but my hands were bloodless and numb. Shirsha was so quiet that I couldn't even tell where she was in relation to me.

'Shirsha?' I said.

'Cut off your feelings,' she said.

'What?'

'Cut them off. Amputate them. Keep them shut away so that they can't get out. That way you never give the beguiler what it wants. It will stay forever, then, trying to get at you, trying to bore its misery into your soul so that it can lead you off and dump you over a cliff somewhere.'

'But . . . but why should it want to do that?'

'Because then it will truly be free. It will be gone, you see, gone from the earth once it has claimed back what it is owed.'

'What it's owed? What do you mean?'

'Is there never an end to your questions?'

I heard her get to her feet and approach me, and I tensed, prepared for anything. She grabbed the rope that held me and hauled me to my feet.

I hit my head on the top of the cave and crouched low to avoid doing it again. Shirsha pushed me roughly across the uneven ground, and I felt the air moving across the face of the cliff as we stepped out on to the ledge.

'You said you would go. Now do it,' said Shirsha.

'Don't push me off!' I cried.

She didn't. She guided me all the way back along the treacherous paths, keeping me safe against the wall at the most difficult parts, turning me this way and that as the path turned. I was terrified, and worked hard at keeping my imagination from showing me the drop only inches away from each step I took. But at last we came to the bottom, and I was relieved to feel vegetation beneath my feet.

Shirsha didn't let me go at the foot of the cliff, but herded me far out into the druze before finally untying the rope and pulling the blanket off my head. I turned to look at her, but it was too dark for me to catch more than a glimpse of her white hair.

She moved away from me and said, 'If I ever see you around my home again, you'll never know what hit you.'

And then she was gone.

I sank to the ground, not caring where I was. My heart was tired from its long hours of racing, and I felt the need to nurse it back to health before I moved again. I didn't know how it had happened, but the beguiler had clearly been reclaimed by Shirsha. I no longer felt any sense of connectedness with it at all. It was a relief and a loss at the same time, but more than that I recognised it as a valuable lesson in beguiler behaviour. But of all the things that had happened, there was one that kept returning to my mind, again and again and again. The minutes I had spent under the power of the beguiler had been a terrible and haunting experience, but it was the moment I had first seen it that kept returning to my mind. That uncanny sense of recognition. What was it I had seen in those golden eyes? What was it that I had recognised?

Suddenly I knew. It made no sense and I tried to deny it, but there was no longer any doubt about it. The creature that hovered in the air at the back of Shirsha's cave was, or had been at some time in its existence, a chuffie.

PART THREE

CHAPTER TWELVE

I sat huddled in my shawl for what remained of the night, too disturbed by what had happened to fall into any sort of proper sleep. Once or twice I dozed, but woke each time with the plaintive cry of the beguiler dragging at my heart. This time, though, I was nearly sure that the sound originated inside my mind, and not outside it.

The same question presented itself to me every time I remembered the golden eyes peering down into my own. How could the distant and anguished beguilers bear any relation to the affable chuffies who were such an important part of our community? Their natures were utterly opposed. Yet there was no doubt in my mind that they were, in some way, related.

At first light I began to try and retrace my steps, hoping to find the little cache of jub-nuts that I had abandoned so readily the night before. But the druze and rhododendron were too thick and I never did find the spot where I had left them.

As I searched I was haunted by the memories of the previous night. What I had seen was surely a form of madness. Shirsha had made her journey and found her beguiler, but in order to hold on to it she had sacrificed a part of herself and was making no effort to retrieve it. She was as confined in the situation as the beguiler was, helpless to escape. It was an impasse, a stalemate, a condition which could not change in any way until one or the other of them conceded. And I was certain that neither of them ever would.

And where did it all leave me, in terms of my own search? There was no way that I could know what had happened to Dabbo on the cloud mountain, but whatever it was had made him too scared to return there. Was I ready to undertake a quest of that magnitude?

There was a raw place in my soul that remembered my brief but unforgettable connection to Shirsha's beguiler. It longed for union again, and that part of me would do whatever was necessary to experience that extraordinary sense of fulfilment. But there were other parts of me active that morning as well; frailer, more timid parts. I had been frightened, not only by Shirsha, but by the power that the beguiler held over me. What if it had led me over a cliff, or up into the snows to die? Could I have resisted it? Would I have even tried? And what use would it be to me even if I did withstand its power, if I ended up like Shirsha; my entire life lived in bondage to the creature?

I decided to go back to my nut tree. At first my only aim was to gather some more supplies, but as I walked along it occurred to me that it would do no harm to put my name on it as well. Even if I did succeed where others had failed, I would still need to make a living when eventually I returned to the village. There could be no harm in staking my claim.

It was mid-afternoon by the time I found the tree. While I was searching around for a sharp stone, I came across two more, much younger trees. They had no nuts on them yet, but in a few years' time they would mature, and I decided to claim them as well. The big tree was easy enough to write on, but it required a lot of care and patience to mark my name on the smaller trees without damaging their delicate trunks and arresting their growth. By the time I had finished the sun had entered its golden phase. It always made me hold my breath when that happened. The forest around me was utterly silent as well, as though all the birds and beasts were aware of the magical moment. The day had reached its peak and was about to start a slow, soaring free-fall towards night.

I longed to be in the village, standing beside the pond, watching the sun's reflection on the dark water, waiting for the girls and boys to return the nodding, bleating herds to their safe byres and sheds. I couldn't remember, couldn't even imagine what had come over me to make me embark upon such a wild adventure, hunting for spooks in the night skies. I wanted to go home.

There was nothing to stop me. The jub trees gave me a license. I might not have succeeded in my Intention, but I had gone one better in the eyes of the villagers. Thirty full-sized nuts would buy a good milking goat. Sixty would buy a yak, and seventy would buy a springing heifer. Within two or three years I could have a nice little business going; grazing my herd on the hill-sides, sending milk down to the plains at first light. Nothing inferred status in the village like material success. Even if people were a bit sniffy to begin with, they would accept me in no time at all once I became wealthy.

I picked as many nuts as I could gather in my shawl and set off to rejoin the porters' path. The going was easy; all down-hill, but my heart was unaccountably heavy and instead of being springy my steps were leaden. I tried to shake off the feeling, imagining Lenko's reaction when he saw my stash, and my parents' and Temma's. They would think I had stolen the nuts, of course, and I would have to bring a party of villagers up to see my trees and confirm my claim. But they would have to admit it was a true find and that the trees were mine. I couldn't wait to see their faces. Mad girl made good.

But none of it helped. There was no relief to be had from the feeling of disappointment that dogged my steps, and I was still bringing it with me when night began to fall.

I walked on, completely unafraid of beguilers after what Shirsha had told me about them and their preferred victims. I had a feeling that I wouldn't see any, and I was right. What I did see, though, soon after nightfall, were the tents of a group of porters, pitched in a broad, flat meadow beside the pathway. It was a place that they regularly used on their way up the mountain and I wasn't surprised to see them there. But I was surprised to see the boy again, lying outside the tents in the moonlight. It must have been the same group, returning with loads from the settlements on the other side of the mountain pass.

I hesitated. The boy was on the side of the camp nearest to the path. For some reason, I found that I was reluctant to meet him again. But he was lying still and after a while I decided that he must be asleep. I crept quietly past.

'Who's there?' he called.

I jumped. 'It's no one. Just me.'

'Oh. Hello, me. Have you got your beguiler?'

I was surprised that he could recognise me at that distance. I couldn't see his face clearly at all.

'No. I haven't, actually. But I've got jubs.'

'Jubs? Good for you.'

'I found trees. I staked a claim.'

'You'll be rich, then.'

'I might be.'

I made to move on past, but he spoke again. 'Given up, then, have you?'

I was surprised by how much his words hurt me. I didn't know how to answer.

'I was hoping you'd make it,' he went on. 'I was sure you would.'

It hurt even more. I realised I was ashamed, and I lashed out in unthinking response.

'Why should you care?'

He sat up straighter and although I still couldn't see him clearly, I had the impression that his gaze went straight through me and saw more than I wanted it to.

'Because the beguilers cause so much fear,' he said. 'And no one really knows what they are. There aren't many people like you. If you give up, then who will go?'

'Why don't you go and catch one yourself, since you're so concerned about it?'

'I can't,' he said. 'I have my own challenges to face. But you could do it. I know you could.'

I turned away, but his words had got through to me. I understood now why my steps on the downward hill had been so heavy. I had given up too easily. For the rest of my life I would have to live with that sense of failure that was already dragging at me. I might be rich, but I would never be happy.

'You don't have to give up, you know,' the boy said. 'I could take your nuts for you and sell them. I know where to get the best price. I'd keep the money until I met you again.'

My mind was in turmoil. I looked down at the warm lights of the village in the distance, then back towards the cold white peaks shining behind me. I took a step closer to the boy.

'I met Shirsha,' I said. 'She caught a beguiler, did you know that? But I don't want to end up like her.'

'Then don't,' he said, as though it were simple. 'Learn by her mistakes. Do it differently.'

There was a moon, but it was behind the tent and threw a dark shadow across the boy's face. All I could see were his eyes, gazing at the mountains behind me. I wished I could have seen him in the light. I thought he might be handsome.

'I'll be a porter all my life,' he said. 'Dragging up and down these hills until my back gives out, or my knees. Everyone's like me, in one way or another. Tied to some kind of daily slog. But you could be different. You have a hunger for life's mysteries. Why throw that away for some stupid jub trees?'

And part of me, that ignored, silent part that had been dragging against me ever since I turned my back on the cloud mountain, emerged to celebrate the boy's words.

'What's your name?' I asked him.

'Marik. And you?'

'Rilka.' I emptied the nuts out of the shawl and gathered them into a neat pile beside his bulging pack. 'Make sure you get a good price for these, all right?'

'I promise,' he said. 'And I know that you'll make it. I'm certain of it.'

CHAPTER THiRTEEN

I spent the night just above the tree-line and listened to the nightangel until sleep overtook me. I felt different about it this time, and I didn't know why. Something that had happened to me since I had last heard it had opened up some potential in my soul and now, as I listened to the varying tones of the bird's declarations, I felt that the understanding of them might, after all, be within my grasp.

I slept long and deeply, and although I was sure when I woke that I had dreamed prolifically, none of the images remained with me.

I got up and took stock of the day. The morning was still chilly despite the strong, pale light, and my clothes were damp from the peaty ground. I beat my arms against my sides and jumped up and down until I was panting, then re-laced my boots and moved off. First I returned to my nut tree, gathering a few whisker-fruit and yellow-pips along the way to add variation to my diet. When I had restocked myself with jubs, I set out again, for real this time.

I kept further east than I had before, determined to avoid another encounter with Shirsha and her beguiler. The peak which rose above me hid the cloud mountain from view, and I would have to go right round its slopes, crossing high above the village. Much as I hated the idea of travelling through the druze, I knew that the shortest route would lead me through its higher fringes. I was full of energy though, despite the steep inclines, and I thought that by the time evening came I would have crossed the face of the mountain and come to the foot of the pass that led across the snows and down towards the sea. But I was wrong.

It took me three full days.

The druze, I now know, is even more dangerous than we had been led to believe as children. I made a severe mistake in trying to travel through it, and should have sacrificed the time to avoid it. Everyone knows that the plants are poisonous and that eating them produces depression and liver damage and sometimes death. But what is less well known is that prolonged contact with the bushes can have the same effect on a milder scale.

No birds nested in the druze, but there was life there. Slow, black flies dawdled around, feeding and breeding on the decaying remains of fallen leaves. Languid grey toads fed on the flies, and they in turn were the prey of the hideous, poisonous toad-worms. I made plenty of noise as I walked to give them warning that I was coming, and it must have worked, because in all the time I was travelling through their habitat I saw only one, sliding away from me.

There were bones there as well, strewn between the creeping suckers of the druze. Most of them were small; the remains of animals that had wandered in there to die, or that had been eaten, perhaps, by snatchers. But some of the bones were larger and less easy to identify, and they added to my unease as I traversed the were-woods.

Since there were no land-marks and nothing but the changing light to measure the passage of time, I don't remember much about those lost days. All I know is that I was constantly wavering between a desperate need to escape and an intense sense of futility. I would have periods of great activity, weaving my way among the bushes and pressing myself through the denser growth, convinced that in a few more minutes I would emerge into the open at the foot of the pass. These would be followed by episodes of abject despair, during which I was equally certain that I would never get out of the druze and I was wasting my time and my energy in making the attempt. At such times it never occurred to me to head downhill or uphill. The best I could do was to sit on the rank forest floor and curse my tainted luck.

By late afternoon on the third day I found myself among thick, tall plants which blocked out all view of the mountainside either up or down. I had long since lost my bearings. My clothes were so saturated with the juice of the black bushes that I could no longer smell it, but I could feel it penetrating my skin and poisoning my body. My water was lasting, but my appetite had disappeared. I knew that I needed nourishment, but I couldn't bring myself to eat and replenish lost resources.

Corpses have occasionally been found in the druze by wayfarers. Some of them have been strangers and some of them were villagers. We were always told that they were led there by beguilers and driven mad, so that they forgot themselves and ate the leaves or drank the juice that flows so freely when the druze stems are cut. But as I sat there alone in the dimming evening light I knew beyond doubt what had happened to them. They had wandered as I had and been unable to find their way out, until finally the poison had overcome them.

I knew that I had to move, to get out of there. Uphill or downhill, it didn't matter as long as I did it now, before it was too late. But when I came to get up I found that I couldn't. There was a great weight like a stone beneath my rib-cage which deadened my legs and robbed me of initiative. For a few moments I struggled with it, then I gave way to despair. All the effort I had made had come to nothing. My certainty that what I was doing was right had turned out to be nothing more than a delusion. Marik's faith in me was unfounded. I was going to die, and no one would ever know what I had been through.

My fingers, wet and sticky with tears, began to stray towards the corner of the shawl where the little bag was tied. A glimmer of hope presented itself. Was this it? Was this the time to open the bag? I touched the hard, bead-like shapes through the cloth and the leather. Would they really work, rescue me in some way from this poisonous gloom? I began to pick at the knot, but as I did so I fell into conflict again. Two opposing voices emerged. One said that this must be the moment; how could anything worse possibly happen? The other urged me to wait, since what could be done now could equally be done in an hour's time.

I vacillated, stuck in the absurd position of believing both of those thoughts. The weight in my abdomen increased, and in an agony of frustration I burst into a succession of gut-wrenching wails and sobs.

I had cried more often than anyone else in my village, of that I was certain. But I had never wept like this before. I wouldn't have believed it was possible. And the worst of it was that now the flood-gates were open there seemed to be no way of closing them again. I couldn't stop. Nor did I have any more chance of returning to my decision about the beguilers' eyes. Even if I had wanted to, there was no way that I could have mustered the co-ordination to undo all those intricate knots just then. The crying had taken control of me. I had no alternative but to abandon myself to it.

CHAPTER FOURTEEN

They seemed to come from everywhere at once, a sudden explosion of noise and activity in the undergrowth that had been so silent. My first reaction was extreme alarm, which took away my breath and my sobs along with it. Then they were upon me; five, ten, twenty young chuffies, lashing their tails and falling over each other in their eagerness to get close to the source of so much sadness. They knocked me on to my back in their clumsy confusion and piled on top of me, pressing wet noses all over my face and jabbering incoherently. Inside a minute my eyes were streaming with a different kind of tears and I was sneezing heartily, but never in my life had the symptoms of my allergy been so welcome.

I turned on to my side and propped up my head with my elbow, resisting the jumping and shoving cubs as well as I could. For a while they continued to jostle for space, like a litter of piglets settling in to feed, but at last they quietened down and relaxed. They were already doing their job, and doing it well for such young things. My heart had been rescued and I smiled down at the indistinct bundles which were draped all over me like an irregular, furry blanket. Then I pulled my bundle of provisions under my head and went to sleep.

Warmed by the chuffies but restless and uncomfortable because of my worsening allergy, I slept fitfully. During one spell of uneasy sleep, I had a strange dream, in which I was floating high above the surface of the earth. I couldn't understand how I came to be so light and insubstantial when I was still carrying the leaden feeling that had crippled me shortly before among the druze bushes. My sorrow was intense and there seemed to be no way of releasing it from where I hovered in the air, but I knew that I was searching for something, or someone, who could free me from it.

In the dream I couldn't see myself. I seemed to have no limbs, no substance at all, and yet I could see all around me quite clearly. Then I hit upon the idea that if I could fly in a quick enough circle I might catch a glimpse of myself from behind. I tried it, but no matter how fast I moved it didn't work. So I tried other aerial manoeuvres, weaving and dodging and doubling back on myself. It was then that I realised what I was doing. It was the strange and complex dance of a beguiler.

I woke with a gasp, fighting for breath. The chuffies had rearranged themselves while I slept and one of them was draped over my face. I shoved him off and struggled against the combined weight of the others until I was able to sit up. It didn't help. I had entered into a full scale asthma attack and I was fighting for every breath.

The chuffies rolled lethargically as I pushed them away, replete with the sorrow that they had removed from me. One or two of them complained sleepily, but few of them even opened an eye. I pulled my shawl from underneath them and began to head slowly and painfully uphill away from their presence and towards safer air. Every few steps I had to stop and wait for a while until I painfully accumulated enough breath to go on. But I didn't put down my bundle until I had put a sufficient distance between myself and the chuffies. Then, at the edge of what appeared to be a large clearing in the druze, I sank down to my knees and closed my eyes.

I was accustomed to dealing with my attacks on my own. Once I was beyond the baby stage, my mother had seldom had time for them. It wasn't that she was any more indifferent or unkind than anyone else; just that mothers in our village didn't have to learn the skills of comforting their children. That was what chuffies were for, after all. And if I was allergic to chuffies, it was my misfortune. My mother did what she could, but it was limited.

So I did what I always did and that was to stay still, concentrate on my breathing, and wait. I don't know how long it took that night, but by the time the attack began to ease off the darkness was faltering and turning blue, giving way to dawn. I looked around me and what I saw took my attention away from my discomfort. I was not, after all, on the edge of a clearing. Without knowing it, without even intending to, I had made my way out of the druze. Above me was the snow-line, with the peak of the mountain rearing away, a paler blue than the sky beyond it. Over its right shoulder, barely visible in the dim light, I could see the shifting vapours of the cloud mountain. The last of the congestion eased from my lungs, and at the same time I got my bearings in relation to the lie of the land around me. I couldn't have emerged from the druze at a better spot. A hundred yards to my right was the edge of the trading route which led through the pass towards the sea.

CHAPTER FIFTEEN

The sun rose and lit the brilliant snows of the pass and the mountain peak beside it. The lightness in my heart was a far more energetic and positive feeling than the sort of smug complacency that the chuffies usually leave behind them after their work. It was the happiness of perseverance rewarded and it brought with it a new optimism for the journey ahead. Now that the asthma attack had passed, my appetite returned with a vengeance. I ate three small jubs, a double handful of squishy puffberries and I kept out a whole whisker-fruit to chew along my way.

I was thirsty as well, and the few drops of water still in my skin were old and stale. Now that the sun was up I could clearly see the channel of a small but swift stream that was running directly down from the melting snows. I tied up my shawl and made my way over to it, then drank my fill with the clearest heart I had known for many days.

The nearest patch of snow was no more than a few yards away, and when I had refilled my skin I walked up to it to mark, in some symbolic way, my arrival at the next stage of my journey. When I drew near to it I saw that it was more like ice than snow; it must have almost melted and been refrozen many times, and was full of black grit. I was slightly disappointed. One of my favourite things about the first of each year's snows is to take a big fistful and chew it, remembering the pure taste of it from the last year and the year before. There was no question of eating this, but as I looked up towards the pass where I would soon be travelling I knew that if snow was what I wanted I would soon have more than enough of it. And at the same time I realised that I was wasting time. A strong porter with good boots could cross the pass unloaded between dawn and dusk, but I doubted that I could. I would need to plan on at least half that amount of time again. That would mean that if I set out now, I would be aiming to reach the opposite snow-line at some stage during the following night. It would be a long, hard walk, but I had no alternative. To stop and sleep in the snows would mean death for someone without a tent or a proper bedroll. I took a bite out of my whisker-fruit and set off towards the path.

I hadn't walked far when I realised that I was not alone. One of the chuffies had detached herself from the wandering band and appointed herself to be my companion. She was so small and so furry that I could hardly see her short little legs, and she seemed to be gliding across the stony ground at my heels.

I stopped and crouched down beside her. She stood on her hind legs and pushed her warm nose into my face, ecstatic at having been noticed at last.

'I'm sorry,' I said. 'I can't take you with me.'

In other circumstances I could think of nothing more delightful than to have this happy, bumbling clown accompany me across the pass. But what could I do? Already my eyes were beginning to itch and sting and my lungs echoed a wheezy reminder of the previous night's discomfort.

'Karumph wither snoggle,' said the cub.

'But I can't,' I replied. 'I can't take anyone.'

'Hickle tarbedis!' she said.

'I know that's true of most people, but I can. I can manage on my own.'

'Affle dandero?'

'Of course I like you. You're wonderful. But you . . .'

She was looking at me apprehensively, wondering what her failings were. I felt like a disapproving parent.

'It's not your fault,' I said. 'It's mine. I have an allergy to you, to all chuffies. You make me sneeze and wheeze.'

She was so disappointed that I felt sorry for her, which was the worst thing I could possibly have done. My sadness attached her to me more securely than any leash and she glued herself against my knees, feeding off my emotions like a child at its mother's breast.

I tried to push her away but it made me feel worse, and the worse I felt the more tightly she clung to my side. It was an impossible situation.

'No.' I didn't realise it at the time, but I was doing what Shirsha had advised me to do with the beguilers. The only way out of the situation for me was to shut down my feelings. I hated it, but I did it, pushing the emotions down and closing a mental door behind them. The chuffie shrank away as though it had been struck. A trickle of regret escaped my barriers and she turned back hopefully, but I tightened the seal and turned away. While I could, I began to walk up the well-worn track, and I didn't look back until I reached a sharp bend, several hundred yards further on.

The chuffie was nowhere to be seen. I was alone again.

The heat was surprisingly strong despite the altitude, but I made good progress and soon found myself in the company of the white peaks, walking along the packed snow of the trade path. Twice that day I encountered porters; one group carrying rice towards the coastal settlements, the other returning with tapestries and silver. They all had tents and must have camped high on the pass, stopping at dusk as was the custom and not emerging until dawn when the danger of beguilers had passed.

When I saw the first group approaching me I hailed them heartily and waved, but to my consternation they stopped dead on the track and looked at me fearfully. I continued to approach and, as I did so, they moved forward again, their looks turning from fear to scorn. Many of the faces were familiar to me since porters travelling that route often stop off for a night in our village. But although I tried to catch the eyes of those I knew, they wouldn't look at me. Nor did they speak to me at all. After they had gone I tried to brush off the experience; told myself that it was their problem not mine. But despite myself it bothered me, and made me feel hollow and alone. When I saw the second group coming towards me I stayed quiet until they had drawn near enough for me to recognise the individual faces, then I called in as friendly a manner as I could. But their reaction was the same; fear giving way to haughty disdain.

I had forgone my chance of returning to the village and was an outcast again. I found myself thinking about Marik, and an image of his strange, dreamy gaze came into my mind. Why had he encouraged me to go on? How was it that he could accept me for what I was when others couldn't?

Maybe I was just a gullible fool. Maybe he was laughing at me now, spending the money from my jubs, buying drinks for all his companions. A dark tide of bitterness rose up under my breastbone, but before it engulfed me a question came into my mind; a question that I had once asked him and ought to have asked again. Why was he not afraid of the beguilers? Why did he sleep outside the tents when everyone else huddled inside in fear?

I had no answer, but the thoughts comforted me nonetheless. Marik and I had something in common. Whatever his reasons he, like me, was unafraid of the night. That fact alone created a bond between us, and although the puzzle continued to nag at me, I decided to trust him. And in the long lonely hours that followed, that simple decision helped me to sustain my spirit.

CHAPTER SIXTEEN

The vast whiteness of the snow was more disorientating than darkness. Broken snakes danced across my vision, never still, maddening in their evasiveness, and from time to time I lost my sight altogether and had to stop and rest until it returned. It was easier to fix my eyes on my feet and I became quite mesmerised by their fluid, monotonous action, which seemed to continue quite independently of my will.

It was nearly dark before I realised that night was falling. The white mountainside reflected all available light so perfectly that I never found it difficult to see the path, even during the darkest time before the moon rose. It was cooler, though, and I made a decision to stop and take a decent rest to refresh myself before it grew colder still and forced me to keep moving.

There was no wind up there that night, and no wild-life of any kind. It was the total, white silence after I had eaten that drove me to my feet again and got me on the move. The crisp sound of my footsteps was reassuring and I relaxed into a sort of hypnotic rhythm, one foot in front of the other. Before long the ground levelled out, and although I expected it to rise again, it didn't, but began to fall away in luxurious descent. Soon afterwards the track dipped down and joined a glacial valley with high, craggy walls. Previous travellers had erected poles or cairns of stones to mark fissures in the ice which ran beneath the snow. The cloud mountain was out of sight behind the closer peaks, which was just as well because I needed all my attention to make sure I didn't leave the path by mistake and end up at the bottom of a crevasse.

Besides that, descending had brought new problems with it. My boots were well-made but I was the last in a succession of owners, and their soles were badly worn. I was inclined to slip easily, so I had to walk with a curious bent-kneed posture which kept my weight steady. It meant that instead of going faster on the way down, I went more slowly, and I was glad when the wide expanse of the glacier began to be broken up by the boulders of the moraine below.

The valley swung round to the left, but the path led up to the right through the snows and I followed it. When I reached the top of the col, the sight that met me made me stop in my tracks. The cloud mountain was rearing above me, in full view now, only its base hidden by the jumble of crags and foothills. I had no idea it was so close, and the prospect of reaching it so soon drained the blood from my limbs and made me shiver in the freezing air.

My mind began to race in panic-stricken circles, looking for a way out. A hundred and one excuses offered themselves to me. My jub trees beckoned, and I might have succumbed to their comforting promises if I hadn't caught sight of something unexpected; something quite out of place in that bleak and windswept place.

At the top of a craggy slope, unmistakable in its stark solitude, was the stone hut that Dabbo had drawn. It stood alone, the only man-made object in the wilderness of snow and ice. Although it was still quite a distance away, I could make out that the door stood open, or didn't exist, and on the far wall the smaller square of a window was allowing the shifting, glinting light of the cloud mountain to show through.

I had to go there. I had to see if Dabbo had left any more clues to his tormented life. But that was all. Whatever I found there, I was under no obligation to go any further. The thoughts reassured me and, wrapping myself tightly in the yellow shawl, I left the path and began to climb towards the crag.

For the first time since I had woken that morning I remembered my dream about being a beguiler high up above the earth. It brought memories of sorrow with it and I tried to evade them, having no chuffies now to rescue me from my feelings. But it seemed as though up here the emotional turmoil I had experienced did not have the same strength. I could remember it and even relive it, but it didn't have the power to cripple me or to pull me in. I played with the emotions in my heart, feeing the sorrow of the beguilers one minute and the light-hearted cheer of the chuffies the next. They achieved some sort of balance between them and it reminded me of the sense of recognition I had felt when I first looked into the eyes of a beguiler, and their undoubted relationship to the chuffies. I was still puzzling over the mystery when daylight began to replace the bluer light of the moon and brighten the snows again. The night had passed a great deal more easily than I had anticipated.

Travelling through the deep, untrodden snow was slow and exhausting. As soon as the sun was up I found a comfortable rock which gave me a good view of the surroundings. It was still very early, and the heat haze which generally rose from the plains and obscured them from sight had not yet begun to form. The views were so spectacular that for a long time I forgot the reason for my detour, and forgot about breakfast, too. On one side, the folding foothills dropped away in a thousand shades of green towards the muddy blue of the sea. And on the other, impossible to describe in its scintillating mystery, stood the cloud mountain.

Waiting for me.

CHAPTER SEVENTEEN

Dabbo's hut was perched on the very top of the steep crag. I was out of breath when I got there, and paused for a few moments before going in. The door was broken; nothing more than a few rotting boards hanging from rusted hinges. But it must have been strong once, to keep out the tyrannical winds that ruled that area even in the summer.

I was aware that there would be a drop on the other side of the crag, but it wasn't until I was inside the hut and looking out through the window that I realised the extraordinary geography of that place. The hut seemed to be hanging in mid-air. Beneath it was a sheer cliff, falling for hundreds of feet. I stepped back, dizzied by the sight. When I plucked up the courage to look out again, I saw more. The cliff swung around on both sides in a long, shallow curve. I could see it for miles in each direction, a massive rock wall like the rim of a crater. I couldn't see the far side, as it was hidden by the shifting vapours, but I had no reason to believe that it didn't continue all the way round, completely encircling the cloud mountain.

Now I understood Dabbo's drawings. How many days and weeks and months and years he had stood on that spot I would never know, but it was clear that he had been obsessed by the mountain and had tried in every way he could to know it. The swirls and dots that covered so many pages were his efforts to represent the changing moods of the vaporous mass. What I didn't know, and couldn't begin to guess, was what he had encountered there when he went in to find his beguiler, and why he had never again mustered the courage to return.

I rested for a while, huddled on the raised slab that must once have been Dabbo's bed. There was no sign of any kind of occupancy; no blankets or provisions, no fuel or ashes. He had not been here for more than twelve years, I knew that, but even so I would have expected to find some traces of his existence. It was as though he had never been.

As my body became rested, my mind began to grow active again and I wondered how he had got down the cliff face. I went back to the window and searched left and right along the rock wall, but I couldn't see any sign of a path. I noticed, that although the bottom of the crater was well below the snow line and strewn with a jumble of grey stones, there appeared to be snow beneath the cloud mountain, shining white all around the shifting, dreaming skirts. It was a strange discovery, but not one that concerned me. And it certainly wouldn't have been the cold that had prevented Dabbo from returning to it. If he could survive up here in this shack, he could survive anywhere.

I ate a couple of my nuts and set out soon afterwards to explore the rim of the crater, grabbing a handful of snow here and there as I went to slake my thirst. That excursion turned out to be a lot more difficult than I had expected. The snow had been blown into dangerous cornices all along the lip of the crater, and several times I found myself sinking into deep drifts which gave no warning of their existence. The shawl kept me warm, but I was making very little progress, and was aware of the constant danger of wandering too close to the edge and taking an overhanging snow-drift plunging with me to the bottom of the cliff.

I returned to the hut and continued on in the opposite

direction, hoping that the conditions might be easier. But it was the same story that way: deep, unpredictable drifts and the ever-present danger of collapsing cornices. I was making no headway at all, and eventually, tired and dispirited, I made my way back to the hut.

Already it was beginning to feel like home. It occurred to me that Shirsha might be wrong, or that Dabbo might have lied to her. Perhaps he had never been to the cloud mountain at all? Perhaps he had found his beguiler somewhere else, and had merely made up the story about going to the cloud mountain in an effort to get it back?

But if so, why had he spent so much time here, gazing out of this window? Of that much, at least, I had no doubt. It was well known that he had spent most of each year away from the village, and the drawings proved that he had been here. What kind of life had he led? What had been in his mind all that time?

I looked out at the mountain. There was nothing solid in its shifting mists, but there were suggestions of shapes in it. I could see how Dabbo could have become obsessed with trying to discern the nature of it, and how his drawings were his own way of trying to express the substance that he somehow felt must be there. But was he right? Or was his vigil a product of his insanity; a waste of an exiled life?

There was no more that I could do that day. I stayed at the window, watching the cloud mountain. When the sun began to set, it sent shafts of pink and gold, which glinted off something in the vapours, as though there were particles of glass floating around in there. Later, when darkness fell, the clouds reminded me of a pool which has had ink poured into it. Patches of blackness swirled and spread through the milky haze, reminding me of the spirals on Dabbo's drawings. Later still, when the moon rose, specks of silver and white danced across the shadowy surface, like skaters darting after nippers on a pond.

I was still there watching when the moon completed its arc across the night sky, and although it wasn't dawn yet, I realised that I had been standing there for hours. I turned away. I knew by now that there was nothing special about me. Shirsha's beguiler had already taught me that I had no particular immunity to the dangerous fascination these unknown creatures exerted. And I had no more desire to become like Dabbo than I had to become like Shirsha. I needed to be careful; to avoid their mistakes and ensure that I didn't perpetuate them in my own life. As I wrapped myself up in the shawl for the night, I resolved not to stare at the cloud mountain again.

CHAPTER EiGHTEEN

Having a roof over my head gave me a sense of security, and I slept well past dawn and on into the late morning. When I woke I didn't get up but lay wondering what on earth I was going to do next.

The edges of the crater were too dangerous to walk around; of that much I was certain. The only other way of getting down that I could imagine was by somehow lowering myself on a rope. Had Dabbo done that? Had he even left ropes there, perhaps? Dangling beneath the hut?

I got up and leaned out of the window. The perpendicular drop made me feel dizzy. There was no rope. Even if there had been, I knew that I wouldn't have been able to trust it after so long. What was more, no rope I had ever seen would be long enough to reach all the way down to the crater floor so far below, and even if one could be found or made, I doubted that I would have the confidence to trust it over such a distance.

Even as I was thinking, my eyes had become glued to the cloud mountain again and I moved away from the window. Sitting around in the hut was going to do me no good at all. I would have to think of something else to do.

I wrapped the shawl around me and went over to the door. Something was moving on the other side of the valley, near where I had left the porters' path. I screwed up my eyes and stared hard, hoping for a sight of a rare snowbuck or an even rarer orgwal, but the snowfields that lay between were so bright that I couldn't see what it was. Then a wisp of cloud

moved momentarily across the sun and the snow fell into
shade. It didn't last long, but it was long enough for me to get
a clear view. What I was watching wasn't a rare mountain
creature, but a chuffie.

My brain seemed to stretch inside my head, as the
realisation came to me of what the chuffie's presence there
meant. If it was true that they came to the cloud mountain to
die, then all I had to do was follow, and I would surely be led
by a passable route. I snatched up a couple of jubs and
crammed them into my pocket, then set out across the valley
on a trajectory that I hoped would intersect the chuffie's
route.

It was hard going, with deep snow and rocky outcrops
causing me to make all kinds of loops and zig-zags and
backtracks. Once I fell into a drift that swallowed me whole
and I had to dig my way out. I became frantic with
impatience, fearful of losing sight of the chuffie, but I needn't
have worried. The closer I got, the slower the poor old
creature seemed to be moving.

But when it saw me, the chuffie acted in a way that I had
never seen before. It appeared to become agitated; it turned
this way and that in the snow, as though it were looking for a
bolt-hole or an escape route. When it failed to find any, it
went on, a bit faster than before and without looking at me.
It isn't in a chuffie's nature to reject any kind of human
companionship, but I was in no doubt at all that I was being
given a strong hint.

I didn't take it, though. I didn't even consider turning
back. Within another few strides I was in the chuffie's tracks
and gaining on it fast.

It clearly wasn't the first of its kind to have come this way.
Even since the last snowfall a large number of tracks had been
made. If I had come across them without seeing the solitary

individual, I might have come to the conclusion that a whole herd of chuffies had come that way. But now I understood that this was a regular pathway, one that, for some reason, each chuffie instinctively followed when it sensed that it was nearing its end.

As I caught up with it, the chuffie turned to me with a mournful expression and I was surprised and saddened to discover that I knew her. It was Hemmy's old chuffie; the one who had been nurturing her so carefully in the days before I left the village. It had been apparent even then that she was near the end. Now it was painfully clear. Her eyes had become dull and had shrunk far back into her skull. Every movement she made seemed to cause her a colossal effort, and I wondered whether she was even going to make it as far as her destination.

I drew alongside her. She didn't stop. I stroked her wiry coat and spoke softly to her. It seemed wrong to me that she should have to make such an arduous and lonely journey at that hour of her life. She ought to have been given a warm bed beside Hemmy's fire and allowed to drift quietly into the beyond. But for chuffies, things didn't happen that way. It wasn't that the villagers were mean. Most of them would gladly have allowed an elderly creature like this one to retire and live out her days in comfort and security. But it seemed that the chuffies didn't want that. One day they would be there, getting on with their emotional duties as usual, and the next, with no warning at all, they would be gone. They were rarely seen on their final journey, but porters occasionally brought reports of having seen them in the distance, making their way across the snows. No one, to my knowledge, had ever tried to follow one. Except Dabbo, perhaps.

There was an edge of pleading in the chuffie's voice as she spoke. I had never heard anything like it before.

'Osgaggy iffygong,' she said.

'I'm sorry,' I answered. She was being polite, but I knew she was afraid that I would drain her meagre resources and prevent her reaching her resting place. Even though I didn't feel particularly sad, I was aware that she was interacting with me, disentangling my cluttered emotions. Neither of us wanted it to happen, but neither of us could prevent it. It was just what happened when chuffies and people came into contact.

'Wimdlety shoffasagus olbappy,' she said.

'I just want to follow you,' I said. 'I want to go to the cloud mountain.'

'Babadiddy werraduff.'

'Why? Why is it a bad place for people?'

But if the chuffie knew the answer she was either too tired or too irritated by my presence to answer.

'Arglespik ink welgry poon.'

It was the strongest language I had ever heard from a chuffie. It was still polite, in its way, but it left me in no doubt that the cloud mountain was nothing to do with me or my kind, and that everyone, particularly the old chuffie, would be much happier if I turned round and went in the other direction. But I couldn't.

'I can't find the way on my own,' I said. 'But I'll keep my distance. You don't have to be bothered by me.'

The chuffie said nothing but gave me a long look accompanied by a long sigh. It was strange, but already it seemed to me that her eyes were losing their habitual cheerfulness and beginning to reflect the long years of anguish that she had absorbed from old Hemmy. I wished there was something I could do to help. It pained me to think of her walking towards her death that way, but my sorrow wasn't going to do anything to help her. Quite the opposite.

I gestured with my arm to send her on her way; anything to put distance between us. She seemed to be moving more slowly and stiffly than ever, but she was, at least, moving. I waited until she had gone twenty or thirty yards ahead of me, then I began to follow.

I needn't have gone with her at all. Her tracks, and those of all the other chuffies before her, were as easy to follow as the main street of our village. But I felt less alone when she was there, and although I kept a respectful distance behind her for the rest of the way, I did my best not to let her out of my sight.

She led me across the snows and through another deep gorge which was angling, as far as I could tell, towards the crater. When she came to the end of it, she turned to her left around a sharp crag and I lost sight of her for the first time. When I got to the corner I saw her again. She was just beginning to descend into a steep-sided gully, and as I got nearer I saw that it was a rift in the crater wall. It was long and deep, but its neck, where the chuffie had entered it, created an easy, gradual decline. I hesitated for a moment, watching the chuffie make her awkward way down towards the gully floor. The snows ended about halfway down it. When I looked along to the end I could just make out the widening beyond it where the floor of the crater began. Further still, a long way off, lay the cloud mountain.

There was nothing stopping me now. I had jub nuts to eat along the way, and there was plenty of snow around if I was thirsty. But a nagging voice kept trying to intrude upon my thoughts, telling me to go back to the hut and come again another day. I listened to it for quite a while, trying to come up with excuses for following its advice. But there were none. Against all my expectations I had been guided to the cloud mountain, and there was no reason now for not continuing.

It took more than an hour, at the chuffie's ponderous pace, to walk down into the gully. Water ran down from the melting snows, and for the last half mile of the descent I found myself splashing through a mountain stream. But the water was sweet and refreshing, and the temperature rose as I descended and, on any other day, with any other kind of errand ahead of me, the walk would have been pleasant enough. When I got to the bottom I stopped for a while, waiting again for the chuffie to get well ahead. Then I got up and followed.

The gully was about a mile long, and well before I got to the end of it I began to get a clear view of the cloud mountain. I could see its snowy fringes and the swirling mists rising out of them, towering above me now that I was so much lower down. When I thought too much about what lay ahead of me, about Dabbo and his madness, and his fear of returning to the place that clearly fascinated him above all else, my knees grew weak and I had to concentrate on the simple matter of putting one foot in front of the other. There was no sense in thinking about it. I had taken all the decisions already. All that remained was for me to actually do it.

The mountain loomed over me as I came out of the gully and on to the floor of the crater. The place was colossal, its curving walls spreading for miles in either direction. The chuffie, still struggling on ahead of me, looked tiny in the vast arena and I knew that I was tiny as well, and powerless in the face of the mystery which lay ahead. But I walked on, one foot in front of the other, covering the ground slowly but surely.

I hadn't worked out how long it would take me to get there. On my own, walking at a decent pace, it might have taken two or three hours. But at the chuffie's plodding pace it took a lot longer than that. I became aware that I might not have time to get back to the hut before nightfall and the possibility bothered me. But I was too far gone to turn back now, and my feet seemed to be working with a will of their own.

The closer I got to the cloud mountain, the more of my vision it consumed. From time to time I had to stop and look back, to adjust my eyes again to the solid and comforting contours of the crater walls, because the mists were beginning to mesmerise me again now that I had little choice but to look at them. Several times I took stock on my position, only to discover that I had covered far more distance than I had thought. The last time I stopped to look around I noticed that the chuffie had arrived at the edge of the mists and that her form was beginning to grow shadowy as she moved inside. I hurried after her, suddenly needing to be close to some other living thing and not to go blindly wandering in on my own. But I stopped short before I caught up with her. Without even noticing it, I had reached the first white edges of the mountain. What I had taken to be snow wasn't snow at all. It was bones. Piles and piles of bleached, white bones.

CHAPTER NINETEEN

There's a lot that I don't understand about what happened on the cloud mountain. The first thing is how I came to go on and not turn back. I know that the shock of discovering those bones filled me with terror, and I made an immediate decision to get out of there as quickly as I could. I don't know whether what happened next was a trick of the mountain itself or of my mind. All I do know is that I didn't get out. I went on.

I touched the edges of the mists, or the mists reached out and surrounded me and, very gradually at first, everything began to seem unreal. Colours were at the same time more vivid and more distant, as though I could see them more clearly but could find nothing to touch and hold on to. Then even the substance that had been there seemed to fade out, so that I could no longer feel the shifting bones beneath my feet; I might have been walking through water or air. That's why I can give no answer when people ask me if there is a mountain beneath the clouds or not. I don't know. And as I went, or was drawn, further on in, even the questions that had seemed so important lost their meanings and stopped asking themselves. I became part of the mists, part of the dream, and the swirling vapours all around revealed themselves as the raw stuff of existence in which chuffie and human and beguiler natures were all mixed up together and indistinguishable. The milky air glimmered with strange lights, and although their perpetual shifting made it impossible to focus on any of them, I was constantly reminded of the shine of beguilers and of the warm, generous expressions of chuffies. When I stood still and listened, there was total silence in there, but whenever I moved, my mind was full of sounds. As though I breathed them in and made them part of me, the lost souls that drifted in the mists made themselves heard inside my head; I became a receptor for the sighs and moans that they no longer had voices to express.

Still I went on, drawn by something that was outside my control. The cloud mountain was quite still; no wind blew in there, and if there were chuffies moving I never saw them. But the stillness was full of energy, like the tranquil centre of a hurricane. I was part of something that my mind could never grasp or explain, but which my heart understood perfectly.

It happened slowly; so slowly that I was scarcely aware of it. My will departed from me, in thrall to the mystical vapours. Gradually, I found my personality softening, losing its identity, opening to the raw emotions of which the mountain seemed to consist. My attention was entirely dissipated, absorbed by the formless mists.

I don't know how long I stayed there, in that beautiful and terrible and magical place. It might have been a day or a week or a month. Time had no significance. I remember darkness coming and going, but the longer I stayed, the more I became a part of the collected energy which existed there, until I no longer felt separate at all. The bones I walked on might have been my bones. The soul of the mountain might have been my soul. I became part of the mists, and they moved through me in the same way that I moved through them.

I don't know, either, what conditions arose to bring about my departure. I remember, though, that from the mists, where nothing had form, a spiralling particle began to dance with a second one, and then a third and a fourth. I watched, enchanted, as the specks drew light from the surrounding air and resolved it into a pair of golden eyes. They seemed to drill right into my heart and plant a hook there, and even as I watched them I found myself beginning to move towards the edge of the mountain.

The next thing I remember was finding myself outside it, as though I no longer deserved its approval. I was moving away across the crater and I tried to turn back, to re-enter its cold embrace, but I was unable to do it. Something else, some other force, was drawing me away. I was regaining awareness of my body, and it felt heavy and clumsy; an onerous encumbrance which was necessary for existence beyond the skirts of the beloved mountain. I didn't want it. I didn't want to leave. But it seemed that I had no choice in the matter. Against my will, I found myself retracing my steps towards the cracked wall of the crater and along the steep-sided gully by which I had entered.

It wasn't until then that the horror of what had happened began to sink in. I had been so totally absorbed by the mists that I had completely lost my individuality and my autonomy. The further I got from the cloud mountain, the more frightened I became of the effect it had produced upon me. Any thoughts of returning created a turmoil of revulsion in my re-established consciousness.

I understood now the reason for Dabbo's fear.

But I still didn't understand why I had broken free. By the time night began to fall I was climbing the last stages of the gully neck. My feet, which had become soaked in the stream lower down, were beginning to freeze in the snows and I was in quite some discomfort. I was anxious to get back to the hut, desperate for shelter and the meagre sense of security it offered, when I first noticed the beguiler.

It was then that I remembered watching it form inside the mountain, and I came to the conclusion that it must have somehow constituted itself out of the miasma in response to my presence, or to my increased receptivity. But at the time when it first became visible in the growing dusk, it knocked all logical thinking out of my mind. All I knew was that I had accomplished what I had set out to do. Like Dabbo before me, I had survived the ordeal of the cloud mountain and emerged with my reward.

PART FOUR

CHAPTER TWENTY

When I reached the top of the gully I stopped and appraised the beguiler. It bobbed and darted above my head, cutting brief comet trails through the dark air, creating a glorious display, for my eyes only. A wave of possessiveness swept over me. It was mine. I had caught it. For a few unforgettable minutes I was euphoric. Against all the odds I had prevailed. I imagined my parents' faces filling with astonishment as they watched their renegade daughter walking triumphantly into the village, beguiler in tow. A flush of warmth drove the cold from my bones and I set out again; a hero, reprieved from mortal suffering by my triumph.

But the impression didn't last for long. By the time I reached the valley where I had first encountered Hemmy's chuffie, my body had begun to feel burdened by a massive weight. Even worse than that was the sense that my mind was similarly encumbered. The snows were bright; the chuffies' path was clear and smooth, but it seemed to be absurdly difficult to stick to it. Whenever I looked up, the beguiler was there, shimmering in its own brilliance, offering delights beyond the drudgery of human endeavour. But something inside me, some stubborn and indefatigable will, made me determined to reach the hut. I sent reverent thanks to Dabbo. If ever I had been contemptuous of him, I apologised for it now. In that vast, silver night, the prospect of the sanctuary that he had created was all that kept me going. And when I did, eventually, reach it, no homecoming had ever felt so welcome or so secure.

The cold slab might have been a feather bed. For a while I lay awake, trying to process the massive amounts of new information that were jostling for attention in my mind. The memory of the cloud mountain brought swift clutches of fear each time I touched on it, but despite the difficulty of my last, short journey, I found I had no anxieties about the beguiler at all. I was positive that I could manage it.

With that thought still sitting smugly in my consciousness, I dropped into oblivion.

The next thing I knew was the cold shock of powdery snow against my face. It was a moment or two before I realised what was happening, but as soon as I did I understood what a fool I had been to have such confidence in my powers of resistance. Even while I slept the beguiler had asserted its influence, and I had wandered in a dream over a surprising distance. It hovered above me now, as I fought my way out of the deep snow-drift, its bright eyes boring into mine, compelling me to get up and start moving again. But I could tell this time where it was trying to take me. My footprints led away from the door of the hut and angled sharply back, taking the smoothest and quickest route towards the sheer edge of the crater. Another few yards and it would all have been over for me.

The fright galvanised me and, with a colossal effort, I turned my back on the beguiler and began to labour back through the snow towards the hut. Every step was an ordeal. It seemed as though my innards were harnessed to a boulder which I had to haul uphill, like the man in the story who displeased the gods. But I was driven by a fear that was stronger than the power of the beguiler and though my heart was galloping like a hunted hare, I made it back to the hut.

When I got there I remembered the length of gut that had

been part of Dabbo's equipment. I needed it now, and I used it immediately, tying one end around my ankle and the other to one of the door's rusted hinges. I don't know what qualities that little length of cord had but, like the shawl, it did what Dabbo had promised it would. When I eventually succeeded in quieting my heart I sank back and closed my eyes; slept again, or perhaps got up and walked; sleep-walked back to the cloud mountain. Now there were sounds there; the spine-chilling howls of beguilers, the cries of forsaken travellers carried on the wind, my own voice, calling desperately for help. I was still calling feebly when I woke, my breath constricted by fear.

Outside the open door I could see particles of snow in the air. It might have been loose flakes tossed up by a breeze, or it might have been a light blizzard. Either way it gave me the excuse to do what I wanted to do, which was to stay exactly where I was. I needed rest.

Throughout what remained of the day, I stayed wrapped up in the shawl, slipping in and out of sleep, my thoughts and my dreams running into each other. None of them cast much light on my situation, but I remember that during one spell of clarity I came to understand something about my society's responsibility in the whole, strange situation. By trying to avoid distress; by allowing the chuffies to soak up all our sorrow and anger and upset, we created the beguilers.

I now know that it was true that chuffies travelled to the cloud mountain when they were too worn out to serve our purpose any longer. It was true that they died there, or at least they left their bones to spill out around the edges of the mist. But that wasn't the end of them. In some strange way they became part of the mountain, adding their accumulation of anguish, and when there was enough of it in there to create imbalance, a beguiler was born. It could be said that they were the souls of chuffies, returning to human society to demand the payment of debts. That was why they led people to their deaths. An eye for an eye. A life for a life. The beguilers were bound to the mountainside until they had claimed their payment. After that they disappeared, or were released; to where and to what there was no way of knowing.

And I, now, was bound to a beguiler. I couldn't imagine how I had ever been such a fool as to think that I would succeed where so many others had failed. And the more I thought about it, the more afraid I became. As the day wore on, the same thoughts returned to torment me again and again and, no matter which way I turned them, I found that there were only two possibilities open to me. The first was to become as deranged as Dabbo and Shirsha. The second, the escape route, was to die.

Compared to life-long misery, death seemed to me to be preferable. Who would miss me, after all? What had I to live for? There would, at least, be one less beguiler to harass the villagers and the travellers on the mountainside. But I was rescued from my self-destructive tendencies by a new realisation. Perhaps I did have reason to live. I had learnt something new; the relationship between chuffies and beguilers, and I surely had a responsibility to pass it on. If I could succeed in returning home without losing my mind, I could tell the other villagers about it. What they chose to do with the knowledge was not my concern, but I had to try and reach them.

CHAPTER TWENTY-ONE

I was awake long before dawn, but I didn't make a move; didn't even uncover my head, until the sun was well up and the beguiler had faded into invisibility. But as I left the hut behind me, I was immediately aware of its influence, trying to pull me back towards the crater wall.

Cut off your feelings, Shirsha had said. I understood now that it was the only protection I had. If I could erect a barrier in my mind that would protect me from that dreadful weight of sorrow, I could resist the beguiler's power and move more freely.

It was like constructing a wall of sand against a rising tide. There was no way of making a strong, permanent barrier. Instead I was engaged in a constant process. I built, and the beguiler undermined. It was exhausting, but I was at least making some measure of headway across the snows. At the bottom of the steep escarpment which led up to the porters' path, I stopped for a rest and ate two nuts. With the strength they gave me, I succeeded in scaling the crag and struggling on up to the track. It was a significant milestone; an achievement to have made it even that far, but I couldn't allow myself any self-congratulation. The well trodden path was quite clear, but how much progress I would be able to make along it was not clear at all.

I stopped again and looked down into the valley below me. I could see the grey smoke of cooking fires rising from a porters' lodge a mile or so below the snow line. The men would probably have started out already, but if there were any on the trail behind me they were hidden from view by its numerous hills and bends.

The homely sight of the buildings tempted me. In a couple of hours of easy walking I could be there with them, trading my remaining nuts and buying a hot meal. Would people know that I had a beguiler, even though they couldn't see it? Not immediately, perhaps, but they would if I stayed until nightfall. What if it led someone else off, having failed with me? For an instant the thought was a lifeline to me; a certain solution to the mess I was in. Shirsha's beguiler had seemed keen to have a try at me, after all. No matter how attached to someone a beguiler might appear to be, it is an illusion. That was why Shirsha lived alone and feared the company of others. Inside twelve hours I could be free of my torment and walking home, unburdened and happy.

I watched the smoke fanning out above the lodges and knew that I couldn't do it. A wave of passion, stronger than any logic, swept through me. No matter how many problems it might be causing me, the beguiler was a beautiful thing. And it was mine.

I took out another jub and ate it on the march, falling into a dogged rhythm as I climbed up the packed snow of the track. After a while I realised that I was moving much more freely than I would have expected to. The beguiler wasn't exerting the same kind of drag on me as it had before, and I wondered what had happened. Maybe the third nut had given me extra strength, or the beguiler was somehow weakened by the strong sun blazing down on to the mountainside. Maybe I had at last achieved mastery over the thing and could now do as I wished. I began to feel optimistic, and wondered whether the worst might not be behind me after all.

I walked on, making surprisingly light of the climb. Ahead

of me I could see the top of the pass, and at my current speed I was going to make it in good time to begin the descent while the light was still strong. I mightn't make it all the way out of the snow that day, but if I was overtaken by darkness I would cross that bridge when I came to it.

My heart was soaring, so full of exuberant optimism that I was completely off guard when I found myself walking along a ridge of crumbling snow that overhung the precipitous edge of the mountain. I scrambled back; flung myself flat on my face as the thin, icy crust gave way. My feet were dangling out over empty space. I was so close to the edge that I didn't dare move; hardly dared breathe. But even in those desperate moments I found myself able to reflect on how clever the beguiler had been. It had been helping me up the hill, lulling me into a false sense of security. Then, while I strolled along with my head in the clouds, it had led me a full twenty yards from the path. I had walked through deep, untrodden snow to get there without any awareness of doing it.

Inch by inch, I dragged myself on my belly through the snow. It was coated with a thin layer of ice which broke into tiny sharp fragments as I crawled through it. When I finally found the courage to get to my feet, my hands and arms were scratched and reddened. With weak knees I made my way back on to the path. I was afraid to stand still because of the cold, and afraid to go on in case I was lured back to that terrifying brink. The compromise I came to was a sort of crab-like shuffle which allowed me to keep my eyes on the place where the land dropped away. Even that didn't work. Within minutes I found that my mind was wandering again and my feet along with it. Time after time I found myself approaching the brink, and time after time it was only with a supreme effort of will that I escaped and regained the path. Eventually, exhausted and afraid, I threw myself down in a patch of snow on the safe side of the path and closed my eyes.

My spirit was as hollow as a drum. I wasn't going to make it. That was all I could think. I wasn't going to make it. Dabbo and Shirsha weren't weaker than me; they were stronger. They had resisted their beguilers' efforts to lead them over the edge. But I couldn't. If I went on, I was surely walking straight towards my death.

I longed for Dabbo's hut. I might have headed back towards it, driven by my terror, but a sound intruded into my confused consciousness. I could swear that I felt the beguiler's frustration as it backed off. As the sounds came closer, I recognised the steady crunch of oncoming footsteps.

I knew that it was a group of porters, but I didn't dare look up. What could they do for me, anyway, apart from giving me a brief respite from the beguiler as they passed? I felt their eyes on me; heard the secretive murmur of words that I might have understood if I had dared to listen.

I looked out and saw the first pair of feet walking past on the furthest edge of the track, as far from me as possible. Some of the men were still talking under their breath, and I knew they were saying awful things about the mad girl crouching like an animal against the hill-side. But before the last of the men had passed me I heard another voice close by; one that was unexpectedly familiar.

'Where?' it said. 'Where is she?'

Almost simultaneously I felt a soft touch on the side of my head and I looked up. It was Marik, and the minute I saw him I understood why it was that he slept outside the tents at night and had no fear of beguilers. I had never seen him properly before but now, in daylight, it was all quite clear. His pale eyes were looking towards me, but not at me. There was life in them, and energy, but no sight. Marik was completely blind.

I stood up and took his wandering hand.

'You made it?' he said.

'I haven't made anything,' I said. 'I have a beguiler, but I can't . . .'

The truth about the position I was in came home to me and I choked back tears.

'Can't what?'

'I can't get home. It keeps trying to pull me over the edge. I don't think I have enough strength to resist it.'

Marik was still holding my hand. Now he let it go and pulled the headband of the heavy load up over his forehead. He crouched quickly, and let the sack down gently in the snow.

'What are you doing?' said one of the men. The others had gone on ahead, but he was hanging back, waiting for the boy.

'You go on,' said Marik. 'I'll catch up with you when I can.'

'You will not,' said the man, in a threatening tone. 'You'll heft that load again and get back on the trail.'

Marik shook his head and turned back to me. 'I have something for you.'

He put his hand into his pocket and I heard the heavy jingle of valuable coins.

'You sold the jubs?'

But before he could answer the man had returned to his side and launched an attack upon him. His clenched fist was like a lump hammer and Marik had no way of knowing that it was coming. He staggered sideways and fell over his pack, landing on his face in the snow. Without even knowing it, I was on my feet and launching myself like a cornered snatcher at the porter.

He could have swatted me like a buzz-bat, but he didn't. It seemed crucial to him to stay out of my reach, as though I carried leprosy or some other dreadful infectious disease. I stood between him and Marik, and although he swore and tried to order the boy back to work, he didn't dare come any closer. Eventually he hurled a last mouthful of obscenities at Marik, turned on his heel and set out after the others.

Marik got to his feet. He had a nasty red mark on his cheekbone, but otherwise he seemed unharmed. He smiled at where he thought I was and I stepped round in front of him.

'I hope you haven't lost your job.'

'We can worry about that later,' he said. 'The first thing we have to do is to get you home.'

He felt around in the air beside him until he found his pack, then he opened it. He took out a thick shawl for himself and a spare jumper, which he threw in my direction. From a side pocket he pulled a long thin cotton scarf and a packet of food, which he set about opening immediately.

'My mother's cooking,' he said. 'Butter-rice and some cinnamon bread. Good for energy. We ate at the lodge last night so I didn't need this.'

The rich oil from the butter-rice was leaking through the papery leaf and the sight of it made my mouth water.

'Eat,' he said.

I didn't need to be asked twice. I pressed him to share it with me, but he declined, and stood with a satisfied smile on his face as I wolfed down the first cooked food I had eaten since I left the village. It was cold and soggy, but it was still the best meal I had eaten in my life and I didn't leave a scrap of rice for the black corbies who circled us in the heights.

Marik was feeling around in the snow. 'Can you see my stick?' he said.

I retrieved it for him and put it into his hand. He parked it under one arm and began to unwind the cotton scarf. 'One end around your wrist,' he said. 'And the other around mine.'

I helped him tie the knots, but I wasn't at all sure what we were going to do next.

'I don't know if this is a good idea,' I said. 'I'm not going to be much of a guide to you. The beguiler is likely to pull us both over the edge.'

Marik laughed and shook his head.

'I learnt to tread these paths like this,' he said. 'Coupled up to my father. But I don't need it any more. I know the mountain way inside out. I can feel the path with my feet, you see.'

I couldn't believe my luck. The only person in the world who could have helped me had come along at exactly the right moment. Perhaps there were forces working with me as well as against me.

CHAPTER TWENTY-ONE

For the first stretch I concentrated hard, watching Marik like a hawk in case he made any errors on the path and keeping the scarf loose between us. But it didn't take long for Marik to prove that he knew the mountain path inside out. He trod it easily, feeling ahead with his stick and keeping to the dead centre. He was strong and fit from months of portering, and he told me that without his load he felt like a brindlehound that had slipped its leash. He strode on up the mountainside with ease and confidence, and seemed as happy as I was about the sudden change in our circumstances.

But after a while the pace he was setting became too much for me, and I began to drag behind like a reluctant child. He slowed to make things easier for me, but by then I was beginning to take his lead for granted and, as my concentration became less focussed, the beguiler began to tug at me again. I would wander in Marik's steps for a while, then gradually begin to waver and move towards the edge, so that he had to haul me in beside him. If anyone had seen us from a distance they would have thought I was the one that was blind.

We made the top of the pass by dusk and, although the gathering dark made no difference whatsoever to Marik, it made me anxious. I knew that the beguiler's power would be intensified in the night, and although I trusted Marik, I was still uneasy about not being able to see where we were going. I suggested that we stop and, reluctantly, Marik agreed. Wrapped in our shawls, we huddled together in the scant shelter of a clutter of boulders beside the path. I gave Marik a jub and helped him to crack it against one of the rocks. He beamed with delight when he tasted it.

'So that's why they make such a fuss about these things,' he said.

'Haven't you ever eaten one before?'

'Where would I get a jub nut? On the wages I earn?'

'But you had all mine. Are you telling me that you didn't even eat one?'

He seemed appalled by the idea. 'Of course I didn't!' He felt in his pocket again and pulled out the coins.

'You look after them, Marik,' I said. 'We'll divide them when we get to the village.'

His face darkened. 'I'm not doing this for money,' he said. 'I don't want it, all right? I don't want any of it.'

'All right,' I said. And then, after a pause, I went on, 'Why are you doing this then?'

'I don't know,' he said, softly. 'There are things in the world, and people too, who are just, somehow . . . right. Do you know what I mean?'

I wasn't sure I did.

He went on. 'It's not that they're better, or more holy or anything like that. You know the way wild fruit in the forest is always more satisfying than what the farmers grow. It's not bigger or sweeter. It's just right. What it ought to be. That's what I felt when I first met you. You were authentic; you were true to something within yourself that no one else could hear. And even if everyone hated you and feared you, you were going to follow your own path.'

I thought it sounded a bit grand, but I didn't say anything.

'I always wished that I would get a calling like that,' Marik said. 'Ever since I was a child I listened and waited for the opportunity to come my way. To prove myself. Not to anyone else, but to me.'

'Now you have,' I said.

He smiled. 'Now I have,' he said.

We are taught never to go to sleep in the snow, no matter how tired we are. We all learnt the story of the snow wizard who steals the breath from all living things who forget to look after it, and we know that it happens, too; that people who get caught in the snow grow tired and go to sleep and never wake up again.

I tied Dabbo's twine between my ankle and a jutting rock. Before I had finished, Marik was sound asleep, wrapped up tight in his jacket. I was too excited to be tired, and I resolved to stay awake and keep my guard well up against the beguiler. But my exhaustion overcame me within a few minutes of settling down, and when I woke, some hours before dawn, I knew for certain that the snow wizard was only a story.

But the beguilers weren't. The moon must have been new while I was among the mists of the cloud mountain, for now it was waxing. It gave good light, particularly up there among the snows, but it was not enough to hide the beguiler.

It was the first thing I saw when I sat up and looked around. It was hovering between where I lay and the path, as though it had been there all night, waiting for me to wake up, faithful as any chuffie. I turned my eyes away from it and checked the twine on my ankle and the rock, then reached for Marik's stick. I knew that the stick had no power to protect me, but it was comforting to hold it and know that I was no longer alone.

There were still so many questions that I couldn't answer. What were the creatures made of and how did they survive? Did they eat, and if so, what? Or was their only hunger the one which needed a human life to be satisfied? Gripping the stick with both hands, I studied the beguiler. It stared unblinkingly into my eyes for several seconds, and then it began to dance. As I watched, I knocked the end of Marik's stick hard against my chest, hoping that the physical discomfort would help to protect me against mesmerisation. But this time I seemed to have no desire to follow. Instead, I was pulled into the dance itself, remembering my dream and how, when I was the beguiler, the reason for the dance had been to see myself. Was it so with this one? Did it dance in the effort to get round behind itself and learn to know what it was?

And how, I wondered, did it see me? Did I appear just as I was, a human figure, four-square, solid as the rest of the world around? Or was it, in some way, only my soul that it perceived, or my life, the way a snatcher senses only blood and doesn't have much awareness of who owns it. As I watched, I realised that although the beguiler was unlikely to leave me, I hadn't really caught it at all, not in the way that I had intended. I'd had an idea that I would contain it in some way and bring it back in a bottle or wrapped in my shawl so that we could study it and find out what it was. As I thought about that, I noticed that the beguiler's dance was bringing it steadily closer to me and an idea began to form in my mind.

It was freezing up there. My breath was like a dragon's, leaving me in great smoky plumes which dispersed in the air above my head. But the jumper that Marik had lent me meant that I could afford to take the shawl from around my shoulders, at least for a while. As I took it off and straightened it out, I moved nonchalantly, the way I would if I was sneaking up on a young lamb that was reluctant to be caught. The beguiler continued with its dance as I began to prepare the shawl. The gut was already out of it, tied securely to my ankle. I unwrapped the little leather bag and tied it by its thongs around my wrist, so that the four corners of the shawl were empty. As casually as I could, so as not to arouse the beguiler's suspicions, I laid the stick aside. Without looking, I made four hard snowballs and knotted them into the corners of the shawl. Then I took one in each hand and waited until the beguiler's dance brought it right before my eyes. As it darted away again, I threw the shawl up and over it.

I swear my aim was good. The cloth covered the beguiler and hid it for a moment. My mind was inflated by triumph, then flattened as it was confronted with the impossible. The beguiler came straight through the shawl as though it hadn't been there at all. It hovered before me again, disdainful of my foolish tricks. In a combination of rage and desperation I leapt up and made a grab for it. When I imagine it now, I see the light being squeezed out between my fingers like soap-nut bubbles. But that wasn't what happened. It just came through my hands the way it had come through the cloth of the shawl, pure spirit seeping through the mesh of matter.

Could nothing hold it? I was seized by a sudden, over-whelming fury and all caution left me. I lunged at the beguiler again and came crashing down on to my face as the gut caught me in mid-air. I was ten feet from where I had started and badly winded. I had taken a knock on the head and my chest was bruised from the fall, but I was alive. As I came to my senses I realised that I wouldn't have been if it weren't for the gut. And, more importantly, I knew that I had deceived myself about the beguiler's power over me. I had thought I could resist it, play with it, take chances, but I had been dangerously wrong. As though to prove my point it came and danced engagingly before my eyes, then did a swooping circle around the ankle which was tied before taking up position in front of me again.

My heart filled with yearning as I looked into its golden eyes. It was so beautiful and I had deceived it; tried to take it captive, as though it wasn't already. I held a terrible weight of responsibility, having brought this spirit creature from the cloud mountain, but I was failing it, every hour that I remained alive. It wasn't mine. I couldn't hold it, and yet I was holding it, just by being there. I was gripped by a powerful longing to release it, and be released myself from this misery. All I had to do was to cut that stupid piece of gut, then all my ties with the earth would fall away. We would be liberated, both of us.

But for what? The emptiness beyond the edge of the precipice filled me with dread. It would be free fall, into nothingness, into the unknown. What if nothing existed beyond that? Who could ever know where the beguilers go once they have reclaimed the soul that is owed to them? This existence of mine was full of pain and confusion, but it was all I could be sure of. I might feel that life was not worth living, but what was the value of dying?

The white mountain stretched up above me, glistening in the early light. I don't know how, but I was aware that Marik was awake. He said nothing, but there was communication even in our silence. Some inner vision that he had enabled him to understand me in a way that no sighted person did. And, I realised, I understood him in the same way. We had recognised it the first time we met. Despite the complexities of our natures and differences in our origins, there was something that connected us.

As I tied the scarf between us again, ready for the next stage of the journey, the little bag rattled at my wrist. I decided to leave it there so that I could get at it easily. The beguiler had already shown me how cunning it could be and I was determined not to take anything for granted.

CHAPTER TWENTY-TWO

'What are you going to do with it?' said Marik. 'When you get there?'

'I don't know.' Now that I had his help some of my most immediate worries had receded. But that one remained at the back of my mind like a great black hole. I didn't like thinking about it.

'Any ideas?' I said.

He shook his head. We were walking briskly down the other side of the pass now and beyond the white snows, still hidden by morning clouds, lay the forests and the drowning pool and the village. I told him all I knew about Dabbo and Shirsha and his face took on a look of concern. He felt along the scarf and, just briefly, took my hand in his.

'You mustn't end up like them,' he said.

'I don't intend to. Not if I can avoid it.'

'You will,' he said. 'I know you will.'

I wished I had as much faith in myself as he seemed to have.

'Will you stay with me, Marik? Until I work out what to do?'

His face clouded. 'I wish I could. But if I don't go back and pick up that load I'll never work again.'

He reeled me in urgently as I began to drift towards a nearby overhang, then went on, 'It wouldn't matter to me so much if I thought there was anything else I could do. I made my mind up, you see, that I would never allow my blindness to make me helpless. I wasn't going to spend my life dependent upon others. When I told my father I intended to be a porter like him he laughed at me. Everyone did. But I proved that I could do it. It's all I've got.'

'Then you have to go back,' I said, doing my best to keep my disappointment out of my voice. 'You can turn back any time, you know? I can manage.'

'I'll take you as far as the snow-line,' he said. 'I can get back tonight and I'll catch them up at the market before they set out again tomorrow.'

'You'll miss your rest day.'

He grinned broadly. 'That's one thing I have in my favour. I'm as strong as two yaks.'

He could have let me go long before he did. After another hour of walking the worst of the danger was behind us, and the path fell smoothly away towards the valley with no more precipitous drops. But I was in no hurry to lose him and my anxiety increased with every step of the way.

I thought of how I might try and persuade him to stay. My trees would certainly create enough income for two of us, and he could carry the nuts to the plains for me, and later, if I branched out, he could deliver my milk. But somehow I knew that we were neither close enough nor distant enough to come to an agreement like that. He wouldn't accept a gift of partnership, I knew, and nor could I offer to be his employer without offending him.

And there was another thing, too. I was growing fond of Marik; I wanted him to be a friend forever. But although he had helped me, saved my life perhaps, he wasn't responsible for my problem. I had embarked upon this mission alone and, one way or another, I had to find a way to finish it. If I succeeded, then Marik and I could start afresh.

If.

All too soon we descended into thinner snow. Stones and dormant vegetation began to show through on the path, and Marik had to slow down and pick his way more carefully. I hadn't done it on purpose, but I noticed that I was taking the lead more and more often and, if I had stopped to think, I might have realised that I needed Marik's help more than ever. But I didn't. It seemed to him that he was not needed any more, and before we reached the snow-line he stopped in the path and told me that it was time for him to go back.

I could have cried. Instead I turned towards him and began to untie the scarf that bound us together.

'Will you stop in the village on your way back?' I said.

He nodded.

'Promise?'

'I promise.'

He gave me the money from his pocket. I tried to persuade him to keep some of it, but he wouldn't.

'Next time,' I said.

'Next time,' he said.

Suddenly we were in each other's arms, and it felt to me as though I had spent my life searching for that moment. The brief embrace was home and safety and warmth, and it exposed my closely guarded heart the way a wing-tail digs out a ground plum; gently, without damaging it. For a few glowing moments I felt on top of the world. Then we broke apart, Marik turned back to the trail, and the beguiler moved in.

I felt its sinister influence the minute Marik began to move away from me. It was broad daylight and I couldn't see it at all, but I could sense it dragging at me, tapping in to my exposed feelings, exerting a terrifying downward drag upon my spirit.

I wanted to call out to Marik; bring him back to me before it was too late. But he had already risked too much to help me. I was struck by the thought that if he came back, I would somehow be allowing the beguiler to enslave him as well; indirectly perhaps, but no less decisively. I couldn't let that happen.

So I stood up and began to stumble down the path. The going was treacherously steep, but although I tried to take my time, I found myself racing and slithering over the ice. I put it down to tiredness and lack of co-ordination, but I ought to have known that it was more than that. I ought to have had more sense.

Within an hour I had left the snow-line behind and skidded and stumbled down the scree into the druze. My descent became more and more reckless. I burst through the undergrowth, tumbled down banks, and didn't stop until I rolled, exhausted, on to a level, swampy ledge. My heart was pounding and my breathing rasped in my throat, quite uselessly it seemed, because I couldn't get enough air.

I pulled the folded shawl around my shoulders, for comfort rather than warmth. As I snuggled down to rest, or to die, or to see what happened next, I realised that there were an awful lot of things I didn't know. Like the satisfaction people got from living normal lives. Like the wisdom of the elders in persuading people not to go off hunting beguilers.

As my mind began to drift again, I felt the leather bag resting against the heel of my hand, still bound to my wrist. Perhaps it was now? Perhaps the beguilers' eyes were the only things that could release me from this horror? I began to fumble with the thongs, no longer caring whether the time was right or not. I wanted to save myself, and to save the village below me from the horror that I was about to visit upon them. But the knots were too tight, my fingers were too thick and stiff, and my mind was drifting into a kind of a daze.

Derisive voices were in the air around me.

'Not her parents' fault. Decent people . . .'

'. . . child like that should have been drowned at birth.'

'. . . saved everyone a lot of trouble.'

Temma was screaming. I wanted to tell her it was all right; it was just me, just me, the same as ever . . .

'By the power invested in us by the Books . . .'

'. . . because it is not the demon you have brought, but the demon you are.'

I was climbing up out of the well, dragging myself like some slow, cold-blooded thing which left a slimy trail behind it.

I was terrified into alertness again and was immediately plagued by a gnawing hunger, as though my famished body had started living off tissue that couldn't be spared. I would have to find food but I was too afraid to move. I lay among the druze and listened for sounds of life around me. There were none.

Until my beguiler shrieked. The sound stiffened my blood in its course. I hadn't slept, I was sure of that, but in some other way time had passed without my awareness and I had been overtaken by darkness. I groped around for the gut coil; searched every corner of the shawl ten times over, convinced each time that one of them must be evading me, until eventually I had to face the truth. The cord was gone. I could picture it still tied to the rock at my last camp, but I couldn't remember whether I had removed it from there or not.

The beguiler gave its plaintive call again and the sound clutched at my innards, giving me a physical pain like a cramp. I pulled the shawl over my head but the beguiler came and hovered above me and I could see its light through the weave of the cloth, stronger than it had ever been. With a sense of dreadful hopelessness I knew that I no longer had the strength to resist.

I got up slowly, into the darkness that lies upon the earth before the moon rises. The beguiler danced triumphantly, shooting high up above the gloomy druze and diving down again. Then it steadied itself and began to lead the way downhill. As I followed I realised that, if it came to the crunch, I might still be able to resist the final fall, whatever it might be. I still had the bag with the beguilers' eyes. There was hope. If I was following the beguiler now it was because I had made the decision to do so, not because I was beyond control. I could still change my mind.

Or so I believed. When the dawn came I was still following, heading directly down-hill. I had passed through the rhododendrons and entered the forest proper, but although I was aware that there must be birds and insects all around I couldn't see any. Perhaps they were all hiding from me, terrified by my despair or the noise I was making as I crashed through the undergrowth. For I was travelling fast. The beguiler was exerting too strong an influence for me to work out a gentler descent for myself in a series of zig-zags. I was plunging straight down the mountainside, sliding at times on the fallen leaves or running to keep my balance, and sometimes even stumbling and rolling. I had long since lost my bearings and I passed no landmarks that would give me a clue to exactly where I was on the mountain.

But if I'd had my wits about me, I would have known. There was only one place that I could be.

As the sun rose the beguiler became invisible to me. But it was still there and it had built up a terrific momentum. I wanted to stop; kept telling myself that if I could rest for a while and take my bearings, I would find that I wasn't far from the village. But I didn't stop, even though my knees and calves were in agony from the battering they were taking. I just kept hurtling down the hill, dodging trees, jumping brambles, skirting patches of undergrowth.

The shawl caught on a branch and was torn from my shoulders. I lost one of my boots in a crack between two rocks. But there was no going back for either of them. The impetus the beguiler was exerting was just too strong.

And then, all at once, I knew where I was heading and, at the same time, I knew that I had always known. I plummeted out of the forest at the top of the slope of razor-grass and rough weeds which dropped away, almost sheer, to the lip of the drowning pool.

A thousand thoughts ran through my mind, all in an instant. I could have stopped, it still wasn't too late, but the prospect of release outweighed my fear. I would fall, certainly, but I could swim. The sides of the drowning pool were too steep to climb, but there might be a rope there holding one of the leather buckets. I would be able to get a grip on it and climb up or wait until someone heard my cries. And surely the beguiler wouldn't be able to influence me once I was in the water. I couldn't fall, since I would already have fallen.

It was over. It was over. That was all that I could think as I abandoned myself to gravity. My legs went from under me. A fallen branch gave me a crack on the jaw as I fell. Razor-grass whipped at my hands and face, stinging the skin as it scratched and cut, but it was yielding. It gave some cushioning to my fall so that when I reached the lip of the drowning pool and plunged on down, I was, at least, still conscious.

I hit the cold, dark water with a shock like breaking the surface of time. For a moment I forgot everything; who I was and where I had come from. All longing left me, even the desire for life itself, and a white spirit light filled my whole being with a glorious sense of understanding. But as quickly as it had come, the light departed. In its place came panic, as every vein and artery in my body changed gear dramatically and my head filled with a terrible, red roaring. I was still descending, propelled deeper and deeper by the momentum of my fall. Panic gave way to rage as I realised how far I had come and how close I was to losing the battle against the beguiler in this final round.

I began to struggle against the water, paddling with my arms and legs in an effort to reverse direction, but it soon became apparent that I was merely exhausting the supply of air that I was holding in my lungs. With a huge effort of will I stopped fighting and relaxed, praying that I could hold out until the water itself brought me back to the surface again. If that happened I would be all right; I could float for as long as it took to get my breath back, then swim for the rope.

The water rolled me over, turned my face away from the fathomless dark below towards the dim brightness above. The distance seemed infinite, and yet I was still descending. I turned again, then again, and realised that something other than my own weight was causing me to do that. Some current down here in the depths had me in its grip and was pulling me downwards.

I resisted a powerful impulse to open my mouth and pull for air. I had been so sure that I would surface again, but now I knew that I could no longer count on another breath. I may well have taken my last.

The current was buffeting me around, sucking me rapidly towards some unknown outlet at the southern end of the pool. Without even thinking about it, I found myself working at the knot of the bag on my left wrist. It was now or never.

The leather thong had been softened by the water and the knot seemed to have tightened. I tugged at it fruitlessly and then, in desperation, pulled with all my might at the bag itself, hoping to snap the strings. All that happened was that it tightened still further around my wrist.

The air in my lungs had given off all its goodness and was stale and useless like the water that has been used for washing rice. My mind was beginning to crack with the effort of resisting the urge to breathe. I yanked again at the bag, but there was something wrong with it. I could no longer feel the hard shapes of the beguilers' eyes.

I was still grappling with it when a sudden whirlpool grabbed my body and sucked it sideways like a leaf into a drain. Now there was no light, above or below. I was in some sort of channel, being rushed along by a racing current, almost straight down. There was no longer any use in struggling. I had taken on the greatest challenge my life could offer, and I had failed. There was no fear now, just a strange sense of resignation, almost satisfaction, as I gave up the fight and let go.

I was outside my body, watching as it was buffeted along by the rushing water. It seemed like such an insignificant thing, there in that hole in the mountain; the mountain itself nothing more than a bump on a planet which rotated indifferently in the black vastness of eternity. The death of one small human being seemed to me to be of no significance at all.

CHAPTER TWENTY-THREE

I was in total darkness, and for some time my only awareness was of having made an extraordinary journey. I might have been between worlds or beyond worlds. Until I felt stones and gravel shifting beneath me, I wasn't even aware that I still had a body.

It hurt when I moved. I closed my eyes again and drifted back into that other darkness, where everything was comfortable and warm.

When I next woke the beguiler was dancing in front of my face. Since it cast no light around it, I was no clearer about where I might be. For a single, soul-destroying moment I imagined that I had been thrown into perpetual darkness in some forgotten corner of the universe where I would be doomed to endure the beguiler's company throughout eternity. But if that was so, why was there a stream there, licking gently at my feet? I listened, and could hear its smooth movement among the stones. My skin stung where the razor-grass had cut it and I felt as if every muscle in my body was swollen and bruised. But I was alive, without a doubt, and for a while I lost awareness of all else but the simple pleasure of drawing breath.

The beguiler swooped and circled in the air above my head, like a moth around a leaf-lantern. From time to time it dropped down in front of my face and hovered there, its golden eyes full of yearning. I watched it, aware that it was trying to get my attention and then, suddenly, joyously aware that it was failing to do so. Something had changed within me; I might not be dead but I had come through death; I had reached the point of no return and I had surrendered to it. The beguiler no longer had power over me. As though it sensed that I had come to this understanding, it swung down before me once more. I met its glorious golden eyes calmly, neither desiring nor fearing it. There was no connection between us any longer and abruptly it gave up, soared away from me, and vanished into the darkness. At that moment, my worn-out spirit began to revive. I turned myself over and carefully sat up, facing the invisible stream. The leather thong was tight around my wrist, and I recalled the struggle to untie it. The bag was soaked through, and when I felt it I realised that I must have succeeded in opening it, because the little balls were gone and all I could feel were the soft, squishy creases of the wet leather. That would, I supposed, account for my survival and my new immunity to the beguiler. Something spectacular must have happened when I opened the bag, but hard as I tried, I couldn't remember.

I wasn't hungry but I knew I was weak from lack of food. When I ran my hands over my body to check for injury I could feel bones that I hadn't known were there, pressing tight against my fleshless skin. That seemed to be the worst of it, though. Nothing hurt more than a bad bruise would; everything seemed to be working.

I dozed off again, clear of the water this time on a patch of smaller, sandy gravel. When I woke, a dreadful anxiety clawed at my gut. I had been sure that light would come, but still it hadn't. If I hadn't seen the beguiler, I might have believed that I was as blind as Marik. The thought of him brought a warm glow and a simultaneous sense of loss. I missed him. I wished that he was with me. And not only because he was an expert on the dark.

How did he do it? He saw with his feet and hands, and if

he could, then why couldn't I? Carefully, haunted by visions of yawning abysses, I began to explore the space around me. I stayed on my hands and knees, feeling ahead of me, crawling across the stony floor. Before long I came to a rock wall, and I was following it around, inch by inch, when I heard a noise in the air above my head. I ducked instinctively and kept still. A moment later the sound came again; a sudden rasping growl which grew louder as it approached me, changed tone as it passed, then stopped. I knew that sound, but I hadn't heard it for some time. The third time it came I raised my head and listened. Buzz-bats. My world expanded, taking in the space around me and moving beyond, because if there was a way for the bats to come into this hollow darkness, there must be a way for me to get out. What was more, if they were coming home now, it must be time for them to sleep. It must be morning.

As if I had to believe in it before it could happen, the first tinge of blue crept into the blackness. The entrance to the cave was out of my sight, but the light was creeping round the walls from the direction of freedom. Another buzz-bat whirred past my head, then another and another. And suddenly I could see them, first one at a time and then a cloud of tiny, leathery shapes which flapped round the curving wall of my prison and disappeared into the darkness above the stream.

My body was weak from want of food, but my spirit sustained me, growing stronger with the light. Long before all the bats had returned, I knew where I was and with a great surge of delight I leapt to my feet. It was the buzz-bat cave where the lepers once lived. I was barely a mile from the village. My heart reached out, everywhere at once. I found myself laughing and profusely thanking the buzz-bats who were arranging themselves in ragged black clumps all over the roof of the cave. I longed to see my family, old Hemmy, even the stuffy old priests with their disparaging expressions; I loved them all without exception. I had caught a beguiler and gone through hell, but now I was free.

As the light strengthened and began to flood into the darkness, I looked around me. At one side of the cave was the circular tunnel through which the rushing waters of the stream had carried me before they washed me on to the shore. I wondered where it led; what kind of route I had taken between the drowning pool and the cave. An idea began to emerge, but before I could examine it I was distracted by a strong smell of peppernut. Breakfast in the village! I began to make my way towards the mouth of the cave, avoiding the occasional late-coming buzz-bat, when it occurred to me that it was impossible for the smell of peppernut to be so strong when the village was a mile away.

I stopped and sniffed again. There was no mistaking the powerful scent, and I began to suspect that my mind was playing tricks on me. I looked around, wondering if there was some cache of food hidden somewhere in the cave, but realised that even if there was it wouldn't give off that smell. Peppernut only smells like that when it is still on the tree, or when it is being soaked for porridge.

I walked to the mouth of the cave and looked around. The ground dropped away sharply below me and I could see out above the treetops into the next valley. A nightangel was singing. I closed my eyes and listened to it. As I did so I heard Marik's voice reaching out to me in my isolation, felt his gentle touch on my hand, saw his back as he turned away from me and began to cross the mountain; a blind boy walking alone, into the snow, into the night. For what? The nightangel answered my question and I found that I understood every note, every tone, every sigh and every sob and every exaltation. I would see Marik again. No power on earth could keep us apart. Maybe he was on his way back over the pass already. We would eat fritters at Jeppo's, or drink a whisker-fruit brew with Hemmy. Soon. We would walk together without fear in the darkness, guided by an inner sight that only we shared.

The nightangel stopped abruptly, silenced by the rising sun. A striped deer and her calf stood still and watched me for a while, then returned to their browsing. A brilliant blue twister winged through the air and the whole forest seemed to swell and vibrate with hidden life. In that delicious moment, as I savoured the return of my senses and the vivid impressions they brought, I would have forgotten about the peppernut mystery if the smell hadn't hit me again, even more strongly than before. It was close to me, somewhere. I searched the trees, but they were all softwoods; no food trees of any kind. In any case, the smell was so strong that it had to be coming from somewhere even nearer than the trees. I looked down at my feet and the ground all around, and then I began to examine my own clothes. Perhaps there were peppernuts in the pocket of the jumper that Marik had lent me? As I lifted my hand to open the pocket, the smell came even closer and my attention was caught by the leather bag, still tied to my wrist. I noticed for the first time that the tight thong was interfering with my veins, and my hand was red from the pressure of restricted blood.

I searched the ground for a sharp stone and began to cut the thong. Now the smell was maddening. With a shock, I realised that it was coming from the bag itself. As the thong finally broke, I lifted the bag to my nose. There was no doubt about it. I squeezed it between my fingers. There was something squashy in there. Now I knew that the reason I couldn't remember opening the bag was that I hadn't. I opened it now and shook the lump of slimy peppernut mush out on to my hand. There was nothing else in there at all.

I sat down on the ground and laughed. I laughed until tears streamed down my face, until my ribs ached, until I remembered what Hemmy had said about Dabbo; about how he had opened the bag and it had made him mad.

There was no magic in there. There never had been. The magic resided in not opening it; in holding out; in battling through. Dabbo's little bag had taught me that you can't see magic, or carry it in your hand. It could still live in your heart, though. It could put you in the right place at the right time. It could bring you the help that you needed.

It had done that for me.

I stood up, and was about to set out when the potters and their apprentices from the village came along, on their way to dig clay from the pits a few miles further down. They stopped dead when they saw me, as rigid and fearful as the striped deer. I waved cheerfully and greeted them by name. For a while longer they stood, watching suspiciously. If it had happened the day before I might have seized up, afraid of their scorn, but not any longer. Never again. That certainty must have been transmitted to them because after a while they approached and greeted me with caution but without hostility. I answered their questions as well as I could, but I found it tiring, and asked to take my leave of them to return to the village.

They abandoned their day's work to accompany me home. The young apprentices ran on ahead with the news while I made my way more slowly back with the potters. They gave me some of the food they had packed for their midday meal te as I walked, feeling my strength revive bit by bit. I ust look strange, but it no longer mattered to me. As ossed the neat terraces I took great delight in seeing the crops growing there, the way signs of order are always pleasing after times of chaos. I supposed that I would stay in the village, for a time at least. I could make some part of my living from my jub trees, and I would enjoy growing food now, or helping to. If that didn't work out I might turn my hand to some other trade. My life seemed to be spread out before me like the rich parklands of the plain, full of potential. Anything could grow there; anything could happen.

I looked up, alerted by a shout from somewhere ahead. The apprentice boys were returning, racing hell for leather along the network of dusty paths. As I watched them approach, I saw that there was a girl among them, her hair flying behind her as she ran. It was Temma. She stopped a little distance away and stood still, searching my face. Then she shouted my name and flung herself into my arms with such vigour that I nearly lost my feet.

'You're back!' she cried. 'You're back, you're back, you're back!'

Before I could reply, she was gone again, sprinting home to confirm the news, the apprentices hot on her heels.

When the potters and I reached the edge of the village, most of the inhabitants, including the chuffies, were gathered there waiting for us. The priests were standing with my parents at the centre of the wall of faces, but it was old Hemmy who came pushing precariously through to greet me first, wobbling on her sticks. I stopped in front of her, and before she spoke she looked at me carefully. Then she said, 'You did it, didn't you?'

I grinned at her in delight and winked. 'I have a lot to tell you,' I said.

'Then you will come home with me and stay for as long as you like,' she said. 'My house is your house, and it will be your house when I am dead, if you want it.'

I hugged her warmly and looked around. My parents' faces were tense; unreadable. Temma was tugging at my mother's hand, pleading with her to come forward, but she kept glancing at the forbidding faces of the priests and seemed unable to move. My father was holding Jan in his arms. Jan was waving and cooing, but my father wouldn't meet my eyes. I started to go over to them, but the priests moved forward and blocked my way. Their eyes were mistrustful, even hostile, but they didn't disturb my calm. My journey had delivered me to truths beyond their imaginings, and neither they nor their dry old books could censure me now. One of them began to speak, but as he did so, something happened. He must have moved slightly to one side, and in the gap between him and his neighbour I could see along the street right through to the mountain wall at the back of the small plateau. The priest's words were irritating, like the drone of a nipper beside my ear. What I was looking at was infinitely more important, but at first I couldn't understand why. It was just the scraggy hill behind the village, that was all. I had seen it every day of my life and it had never seemed significant before. Then, with a flash of inspiration that made my head spin, I knew.

The priest was still talking, but I hadn't heard a word he had said. I waited until the world stopped going round in front of my eyes, then held up my hand as politely as I could to stop him. Because I had realised during that dizzying spell of illumination that the stream which had carried me from the drowning pool must run down behind the steep mountain wall and right underneath the village. But in all the generations that people had lived there, no one had ever known that. I pointed at the spot that had caught my attention; a patch of greener vegetation hanging on to the crumbling earth. The stream must almost reach the surface there, and the roots of those plants must tap into it.

'There is water there,' I said. 'There will be no more need for us to wear ourselves out at the drowning pool.'

The priests looked at me suspiciously, but most of the villagers were peering at the mountainside and discussing what I had said. They might never believe what I had to tell them about the relationship between chuffies and beguilers, but if I could prove that I was right in this, I would have a better chance of persuading them.

'Come on,' I said. 'Why wait? Let's get ropes and picks. We can work instead of talking, and if we find the water there, then you might like to hear about the other things I have learnt.'

The priests were glaring at me in fury. Behind them, the villagers muttered among themselves, some of their voices curious, others affronted at my presumption. I saw my father walking away purposefully, little Jan at his heels. Lenko had appeared and seemed to be arguing with my mother.

There was a murmur among the crowd and someone said, 'But everyone knows there's a spring up there. Why should we bother with it when we have all the drinking water we need in the well?'

'It's more than drinking water,' I said. 'There's a stream running through there which will water our crops all summer long.'

The crowd was dissenting. I could see several people shaking their heads in ridicule. The most hostile of the priests was watching them, too.

'Well?' he said, looking directly at me but addressing the gathering. 'Will you go with her, hunting water spirits this time, instead of beguilers?'

Someone laughed. Someone else made a feeble attempt at a beguiler's howl. I sighed, becoming bored of the situation.

If I had to go up there on my own I was perfectly prepared to do it. But the priest was warming to his game. He turned to the people now, a bemused expression on his face.

'Oh, come on, now. Surely there's someone here who'll go with her?'

A high, reedy voice like a forest hen answered him.

'I will.'

It was Hemmy. Much as I appreciated her support, the image of her swinging from the cliff face on a rope didn't do much for my case. But she did command a certain amount of respect in the community, and a polite, if embarrassed silence followed her words. It was broken by a second voice.

'And so will I.'

My father had returned. In his hands were a pick and a dimmock and a coil of rope hung over his shoulder. Behind him, looking round belligerently, was Lenko.

It was enough. The priest's injunctions were lost in the swell of voices as the other villagers decided the matter. All at once, people were running for tools and ropes and in among them the chuffies were going wild with excitement.

As I set off towards the nearby fields, Temma caught up with me and took my hand. The eager crowd followed, but at the edge of the village I stopped and let them all pass, remembering old Hemmy and her difficulty in walking. She was still standing where I had left her, heroically fending off her young chuffie, who was trying once again to give her a ride. When she saw me looking she raised a wobbly stick and waved me away. I laughed, and was just about to carry on when I noticed another figure standing nearby, also waving to me. It was my mother, busy restraining my furious little brother. I wanted to run to her; to forgive and be forgiven, but Temma was impatient to be on the move. I waved back. She would still be there when I returned.

The sun was already heating the surface of the ground and I noticed that my other boot had gone missing as well. I must have lost it in the drowning pool or the racing stream. The shawl was gone too, and the coil of gut, and the bag of beguilers' eyes had been dispossessed of its magic promise. There was nothing left now of the things I had started out with, except for the empty bag. I would have nothing to hand on to my successors, if there ever were any. Perhaps there wouldn't be? Perhaps the things that I had learned would put an end to beguiler hunters? But as I walked between the parched fields with Temma I knew without doubt that there would always be people like me; one or two in each generation.

If it wasn't beguilers that they sought, it would surely be something else.